AN APRIL LOVE STORY

Caroline B. Cooney

SCHOLASTIC BOOK SERVICES

New York Toronto London Auckland Sydney Tokyo

Cover Photo by Owen Brown

ISBN 0-590-31858-6

12 11 10 9 8 7 6 5 4 3 2   1 2 3 4 5 6/8

Printed in the U. S. A.   06

AN APRIL LOVE STORY

A Wildfire Book

WILDFIRE TITLES

Chapter I

It began in the high school lobby, while we were waiting for the bus to take us on a field trip.

"This is the first field trip in my life," I said to Joel, "which is not to a museum or a theater, but actually to a field."

"Got your birdbook? Your sharpened pencil for quick sketches? Your binoculars?"

"I am suitably armed," I told him. "Right down to the regulation blue jeans and peanut butter and jelly sandwich."

"I knew I forgot something," said Eve. "I wore stockings."

We all looked at Eve's legs. She wears stockings all the time because her legs are so nice. "They're going to be a little less attractive after a morning of tramping through the fields in search of yellow bellied sapsuckers," I observed.

"Marnie MacDonald," said Mr. Ricks, in the voice of one who was tired when he got up, more tired still at the sight of his class, and due for a long vacation by the end of the field trip. "Please let us not have any yellow bellied sapsucker jokes. There really is such a bird. It's a perfectly fine bird. And if you city types can even tell a hawk from a robin, I'll be thrilled."

"My bird," said Joel, "is the pigeon. Its habitat is the sidewalk, the roof peak, and our dining room window ledge. It is known for — "

"Enough, Joel," said the biology teacher, in his least thankful voice.

"First time in biology the subject has been truly relevant," I said to Joel, "and you get cut off mid-sentence."

Joel grinned. He is a senior, while I am a sophomore, and it is incredible to me that with all the sophisticated senior girls around him — in this class both Kay and Eve — he should be interested in me. But he's walked me home three times, sat in the library and studied with me (sort of) twice, and yesterday he bought me roasted chestnuts from a street vendor near our apartment building. I happen to detest roasted chestnuts. I think they taste like something you'd feed a mongrel dog you didn't like, but when a handsome, basketball-captain senior like Joel has already bought them for you, you don't announce you'd rather have popcorn. Or starve. So I took the little white bag and ate every one, smiling, which just goes to prove my mother is right to say you can eat anything if good manners require it. As long as Joel doesn't take me out to eat at a squid food restaurant, I should be okay.

And then Lucas Peterson came up behind me, tapped my shoulder, and said in his funny deep

2

voice (Joel says he sounds like a newborn foghorn), "Marnie, I have to talk to you."

Lucas is one of these intellectual types with so much knowledge squashed into his head there's no room for a personality. He comes from this rather overwhelming family (I should know; they're my parents' best friends) who do not, for example, say hello. They bid you fair welcome. They do not have supper. They partake of an evening repast. They certainly don't chat. They make meaningful conversation. Verbally, it is obvious that Lucas is their son. Physically, the resemblance is zero. Mr. and Mrs. Peterson might have fallen out of a fashion magazine, while Lucas looks like a street pole recently hit by a car. Due to circumstances beyond my control I have had to associate with Lucas since childhood; today, however, the circumstances were under my control. "Later, Lucas," I said, brushing him away.

"There's the bus," said Joel, taking my hand. "Come on, Marnie, let's get the very back seat so we can be alone."

We clambered onto the bus. Joel took the window, I sat next to him, and the only other seniors in the class, Kay and Eve, sat on the other side of us. Biology is usually a sophomore class, but each year there are a few older kids who couldn't schedule it then: We've got three seniors and one junior — Lucas. It's typical of Lucas to be the only one doing something. I caught a glimpse of him getting on the bus, bent out of shape by a load of books, as usual. I think Lucas has some great fear of being stranded in the

3

wilderness without any reading material, because he never fails to keep a wide selection of books with him: something entertaining, something meaningful, something instructive, and something that requires a pencil, such as a *Games* magazine, and, of course, his pocket calculator. I guess you never know when you might need to find the square root of something. Several people veered to escape his elbows. I swear he has more than the usual number.

Lucas looked at me, and his expression, over the heads of the shorter sophomores, was very odd.

"I think he's got appendicitis," said Joel. "Have you promised to be his nurse or something?"

I laughed and forgot Lucas. Laughter is never very far away when I'm around Joel. Joel detests people who whine or complain. We are both in the select chorus, which is quite an honor for a sophomore, and the way he noticed me in the first place, and it's quite the thing in our school for people with problems to spend a lot of time draped over the grand piano in the chorus room telling our very understanding music teacher all their problems. Joel would never do that. His philosophy is that you should solve your own problems, either by laughing them off, or by waiting for them to dissolve on their own.

I told my best friend Susannah that I absolutely loved Joel's philosophy. "Don't give me that," said Susannah. "You love Joel, period."

I didn't, though, which was the reason I felt so funny when everybody wanted to talk about how much attention Joel was giving me, and about how he was co-chairman of the senior prom and didn't seem to be dating any seniors. I loved being with Joel. I loved being seen with Joel. But I didn't love him in the slightest. I knew because they say — Who is "they"? I've always wanted to meet a bona fide certified "they" — anyway, they say that love is star-spangled and all encompassing and leads to insomnia, and all Joel inspires in me is giggles and a tendency to choke on roasted chestnuts.

Besides, Joel was just as much fun when he *wasn't* there.

Susannah and all the other sophomore girls — and plenty of juniors and seniors — were so filled with envy and admiration that I could bask in it like a sunlamp. "Don't forget," said my mother dryly, "that you can get burned from too much exposure to sunlamps." But I tend to hurry on when my mother is in an advice-giving mood.

"Lucas keeps looking at you, Marnie," said Kay. "I guess he really does want to talk to you."

"Lucas doesn't talk to people," said Eve. "He lectures them, assesses them, or analyzes them, but he doesn't ever merely talk to them. Whatever Lucas wants to say to Marnie is probably fraught with inner meaning."

"Lucas is really pretty decent," said Joel. "He's just so used to keeping a high profile at home, he forgets to get rid of it at school."

"His *profile* is fine," said Eve. "It's his complexion, attitude, personality, and — "

"Hey," said Joel. "Cut it out. You were spotty once yourself, you know. I remember you in eighth grade, and how we used to call you Christmas Tree because of all your red — "

"Okay, okay," said Eve. "I won't utter another unkind word about our dear friend Lucas."

I happened to agree with Eve's assessment of Lucas, but still, it was nice of Joel to defend the guy. Even if it did mean saying something humiliating to Eve. If anyone had said that to me about my complexion, I would have blushed so hard they'd have begun calling me Neon.

Eve and Kay began playing hangman with a three-letter word and Joel and I scrunched up in his corner and talked about whether or not he'd be accepted at Columbia University. "I'm nervous," said Joel. His voice was at that soft, scratchy level just above a whisper, and would have been sexy if the topic hadn't been college. "See, Marnie, Russell was just turned down at NYU, and everybody figured Russell could get in anywhere, and I haven't heard from any of the four schools I've applied to and maybe that means . . ."

What I was mostly thinking was that my peanut butter and jelly sandwich was between his thigh and mine, and the sandwich was getting thinner and thinner, and no doubt the inside of my handbag was getting stickier and stickier.

I became deeply involved in the intricacies of deciding whether to mention this to Joel, and possibly arrange a shift of position, or whether talk of peanut butter would destroy not only his train

6

of thought, but also his interest in me and the possibility that he would ask me to the senior prom.

I decided that if I ate with my fingers spread around my sandwich, no one would notice this pitiful little white, tan, and purple glue I was eating.

That's when you know you have developed a truly deep philosophy in your fifteen years. When your boyfriend is talking about Life, Truth, and the Future, and you are singing to yourself, "Peanut butter and jellleeee, taste so good in my bellleeee."

"Don't worry," I said to Joel. "You have so many activities, you're sure to be a catch all those colleges will want to have."

"But now I'm afraid I have too many activities and they'll say I'm shallow and spread too thin and no different from every jock in the country."

"No, they won't, Joel. They'll be impressed with how much energy you have. They'll figure anyone so successful at eighteen will be even more successful at nineteen."

"You think so?" he said eagerly, as if he really valued my opinion.

Up until Joel, every boy I've ever talked to (unless we're discussing algebra or irregular French verbs) has made me so nervous just being there that my mouth fills up with Scotch tape and my vocabulary retreats to the first grade, so I feature exclusively such syllables as yes, no, uh, or hmmmm. But with Joel I can actually converse. It's really exciting. Susannah says of all the things

7

she envies about me (it's so neat to be envied!) my tongue is the tops. "You can actually *talk* to a boy," she marvels.

"All right, class," said Mr. Ricks sadly. "We're here. Please remember your instructions. Scatter widely. Range through the field and scrub pine. Take a permanent position. Freeze in place. Remain until I blow my whistle. Keep my eyes open for birds and other wildlife. This area is redolent with feathered friends and you should all have a good thick list of birds to recount to me when we return to the bus."

"I don't know about Mr. Ricks," said Susannah, "but very few of my friends sport feathers."

We piled off the bus, and sure enough, as we filled the fields, great hordes of birds flew away. I wrote in my notebook, "hordes of birds." "Birds don't come in hordes, Marnie," said Joel. "They come in flocks."

"Flocks," I wrote. I said, "Thank you, Joel." And then he was gone, running easily across the hummocky grass to a position near a clump of grayish trees with little bent trunks from which point I supposed he felt he could do some really good bird-watching. I found a fat shrub with some dead vines clinging to it, set on the icy soil the plastic mat I made in Brownies eight years ago for just such an occasion, and squatted down.

Within thirty seconds it became apparent that this field trip was going to be cold, long, and boring.

Nature is fine. I'm all for nature. I realize somebody needs to observe the plankton, monitor the food chain, analyze the earthquakes, and invent better tractor tires. And I'm not going to grow up to be a polluter of atmospheres or roadside ditches or anything, but nature is just not my sphere.

I had my own binoculars, because my parents will buy me anything if I can relate its use to my education. I spend a lot of good study hours trying to think of a way to prove that rhinestone-studded disco shoes are essential to my education, but so far I haven't found a satisfactory connection there. Still, I love these binoculars. I do a lot of people- and city-watching with them.

"Marnie," said Lucas Peterson, squatting down next to me, "I have to talk to you."

It was not really true that the only boy I could ever talk to was Joel. Actually, I could talk just fine to Lucas, if you could call it talk. It usually resembled more an exchange of insults. Still and all, I couldn't believe that academically perfect, behaviorally flawless, teacher's pet Lucas Peterson would come up to throw a few insults when we'd just been instructed to maintain silence and not move our muscles.

I looked around carefully. Mr. Ricks had vanished, but probably he was a master of camouflage and was sitting on the other side of my very own bush. Joel was barely visible, trying to look tree-y at the far side of the big clearing. "About what?" I whispered.

"About the move, of course," he said. "And don't tell me we'll talk about it later. There is no later."

"Lucas, what are you talking about?"

9

"The farm, Marnie. Don't be thick. I hate people who are thick."

"I know nothing about farms, Lucas. Don't be difficult. I hate people who are difficult."

"North Carolina," he said. "The farm. In the mountains."

The only thing I knew about North Carolina was that, contrary to its name, it was quite far south. My parents spent three weeks there last summer in the Smoky Mountains and loved it. I was at tennis camp at the time and hadn't even gotten around to reading their postcards because Susannah and I were so busy practicing on the courts. My parents had certainly liked it down there, though, because at least once a month they went back for three-day weekends. I loved that. It meant I could stay with Susannah, whose mother never cares what we do or how late we stay up doing it, as long as we do it quietly.

"What about the mountains?" I said irritably.

"Our parents, Marnie. You and me."

"I'd rather not be paired with you, Lucas. Now buzz off. We're supposed to be bird-watching. I would like to have at least one bird for my little list."

"Over there is a white-throated sparrow. Write that down and listen to me."

"I don't see it."

"Right there, pea brain."

"Right where?"

"I cannot credit this," said Mr. Ricks in a tiny nonbird-scaring, but definitely Marnie-scaring,

10

tone of voice. "Two of my best students behaving in the exact opposite manner from what I requested?"

It was the first I'd known that I was a best student. I apologized quite cheerfully. Mr. Ricks drifted off. I expected Lucas to leave, but he didn't. I considered leaving myself, but my legs were frozen in a crouch that if I tried to get up I'd have to hang onto Lucas or tip over and crawl.

I lifted my binoculars and surveyed branches, sky, and ground. There seemed to be a serious bird shortage. I did locate David, who was studying his wrist. Twice when he moved, the wrist gleamed, so I deduced that David was wearing a watch, and counting the seconds until release from feathered friend study.

Not far from David were two brown-haired heads topping two navy blue jackets. These heads were bent over a book that might have been a bird identification text but which I knew from its turquoise cover was geometry. And since geometry was having an exam last period I further deduced that the heads belonged, in unknown order, to Chuck and Leigh.

There was enough lack of interest in biology to match the lack of birds to be interested in. Every time Mr. Ricks finishes a lecture he leaves a little pause, in case we want to ask a penetrating question or make an intelligent observation. But all anybody says is, "Are you done yet, Mr. Ricks? Can we go now?" Except Lucas. Lucas can always think of something to prolong a class.

11

I scanned for birds again, but all I saw was Holly, poking with a stick at something on the ground that was making her go all fluttery and disgusted. Beside her was Eve, stroking her poor stockinged legs, which looked as if they had had a bramble encounter.

What city types we are, I thought. I was proud of it. A city type was all I ever wanted to be.

One bird flew quite close to me then, and the only thing I could state categorically about that bird was that it qualified for the species because it obviously could fly. I couldn't even guess its color, length, beak shape, or flight pattern. I wrote carefully in my notebook, "bird."

"Junco," said Lucas.

"I am not," I said indignantly. "I've never had anything stronger than an aspirin in my life."

"The bird is."

"The bird is on drugs?"

"The name of the bird, Marnie," said Lucas, chewing the words like rocks, "is junco. J-U-N-C-O."

"I think that's terrible. Why do they call it that? Is it given to eating marijuana seeds or something?"

"Marnie when I consider what the coming year holds for me, I cannot believe that I am going to have to endure it in your company. You are ignorant, completely lacking observational skills, and you don't even care what's happening. I should think you, of all people, would be concerned."

"Concerned about what?" I hissed. I tried to kick his shins but I was too scrunched up. I just seemed to be twitching.

"Let's have a truce, okay? No more insults. Just tell me what we are going to do."

"As far as I know, Lucas Peterson, *we* aren't doing anything."

"You mean you've talked them into letting you stay here? You have relatives or something?"

I took a deep breath and held it, counting slowly. I learned to do that in Sunday School, to help keep my temper. But before I could calmly tell Lucas to stop bothering me there was a sudden burst of birdsong. It wasn't twittering or squawking like most birds. It was a wild, sweet cadence, like a fife, some ethereal descant for a special chorus. The melody splashed on me like a falling flute.

I caught my breath from sheer love of the sound, and when it finally ceased, the silence seemed reverent and soothing. I became aware of the shaft of sunlight warming my back, working its way through the fleece lining of my denim jacket. I began to feel toasted and sleepy. It was a feeling of deep contentment, like August, when nothing needs doing and nothing takes worrying. In a few minutes I'd be back on the bus sitting next to Joel, who just might ask me to the senior prom. Or to a movie. Or at the very least, get me another bag of chestnuts.

"Marnie, do you mean to say you honestly don't know what I'm talking about?" Lucas' voice was full of contempt. If he'd been an ant I'd have stepped on him for ruining my mood. I settled for a killing glare but it regrettably had no effect on Lucas' lifespan.

"Don't you ever talk to your parents, Marnie? Don't they ever discuss things with you?"

"Of course they do," I said irritably, but even as I protested I was remembering my parents saying *Slow down, Marnie, we need to talk, there are some important things. . . . But I'm in a hurry, I told them, rushing out, thinking of Joel and school and chorus and ninety-five things to tell Susannah.*

I lifted my binoculars to focus on Joel Fiori.

"Marnie, you are amazingly self-centered," said Lucas.

I was saved from doing violence to Lucas' body because Mr. Ricks blew his police whistle with a blast so shattering I tipped over. Lucas didn't even notice, he was so busy telling me how rotten I was. The groans, moans, and complaints of twenty-nine people who knew now they could cross bird-watching off their list of possible future careers filled the air.

"My feet are killing me," said Holly.

"Feet!" said Susannah, tottering over to me and helping me up. "I have frostbite of the fanny."

"The temperature," said Mr. Ricks witheringly, "is, as is typical of late March, well above freezing."

"But I saw a redheaded woodpecker," said Chuck helpfully.

14

"Oh, yeah, where?" said Kay. "Caught in the logarithm tables?"

Chuck blushed.

Joel came loping over to me. Oh! how he ran. Graceful as an Olympian. And they wanted us to watch birds!

"What was the bird that sang?" Joel asked Mr. Ricks. "The one like a music box just a few minutes ago?"

I felt a deep pleasure that he, too, had been affected by that song. It was a sort of cement between us, I thought.

"I'm not entirely sure, Joel, as this is a little far from its normal late winter habitat, but I would not be at all surprised if it were the winter wren. Latin name *troglodytes, troglodytes.*"

Joel shouted with laughter. "Sounds like a troll. Lurking under a dark and rotting bridge waiting for innocent maidens." He turned to me, spread his jacket threateningly, and hovered over me. I cowered obligingly. "If you don't watch out," said Joel hollowly, "the *troglodytes* will get you."

Susannah looked at us wistfully. We promised each other in seventh grade we would date together. We didn't understand at the time that boys wouldn't necessarily ask us together. Joel reached for my hand.

And Lucas got between us. "I have to talk to Marnie," he said.

Joel looked a little startled but he said, "Sure. I'll save a seat for you, Marnie."

"Looks like she'll be sitting with Lucas," said Eve. "I'll sit with you, Joel."

"I'm sitting with Joel," I said firmly, and Joel grinned and went on. Eve flounced after him. Mr. Ricks gathered the school binoculars and Lucas and I brought up the procession. I was seething with anger.

"Tell me this, Marnie," said Lucas, not noticing my wrath, "have you ever wondered what my parents' hobbies are?"

"No, Lucas, I can categorically state that I have never wondered nor cared what your parents' hobbies are. If you press me to guess, I would probably expect your father to dabble in oil price-fixing and your mother to be an amateur strike breaker, but I could be wrong."

"My parents," said Lucas through his teeth, "are gardeners. We have a half-acre organic garden in my grandparents' backyard in the suburbs, which they spend every weekend tending. It is their lifelong goal to have a few hundred acres, a woodlot, a log cabin, a woodstove, a quilt frame, some goats and chickens, and a good cash crop like strawberries."

"Lucas, I grieve for them. I fail to see, however, that it is any concern of mine whether you Petersons raise strawberries or not. Now, if you don't mind, I'm catching up to Joel."

"Don't say I didn't warn you."

"You didn't warn me about anything except that your flaky parents want to keep goats. I don't plan to visit their goat and strawberry complex, so what does it have to do with me?"

"Your parents want to go along, Marnie, that's what it has to do with you."

16

I was absolutely furious with him. "What are you talking about?" I demanded. "Go along where?"

"To raise goats. If you weren't so thick and self-centered, and full of your own shallow dreams, you'd have noticed the people around you have a few dreams of their own."

I didn't even bother to laugh at Lucas. The idea of my parents wanting to go to some farm somewhere and raise goats was so ludicrous I couldn't even waste time yelling at dumb Lucas about it.

I ran to get my seat next to Joel before Eve slid over too close.

Chapter II

"You don't need to spend fifteen minutes closing your locker door today," teased Susannah. "Joel has an away game. He can't walk you home."

"Let's go over to my house," I said. "I bought some new makeup with my baby-sitting money. We can practice mascara."

"Pretty soon you won't have time to baby-sit. All these handsome men will be taking you out all the time."

"Susannah, wouldn't that be neat? But Joel and I haven't had a real date yet. He hasn't actually asked me anyplace."

"I can't get over the way you can talk to Joel. So easily. Honestly, Marnie, if it were me, the conversation would be Joel's interesting sentence, my duh, Joel's clever remark, my uh, Joel's probing question, and my hmmmm."

I giggled. "I'm not very good yet, myself. When we were coming back from the field trip Joel kept telling me about the intricacies of various basketball plays, and I was so busy trying to think of what I would say next that I didn't pay enough attention to what he said to be *able* to say anything next!"

Susannah got her Latin book, I got my French, and we both had math and English homework together. We liked having classes together. It was hard to juggle our schedules to match, but this year we shared three classes and next year we wanted to try to do the same thing.

"What did old Lucas want?" she asked.

"Who knows. He was hounding me about his parents' hobbies, or something. I didn't pay much attention."

"Your magnetic personality again."

"No doubt."

We giggled again. Susannah and I started giggling in May of the fourth grade when we were in a sack race together, and we've never stopped. My mother says it drives her berserk. You're supposed to outgrow that giggly stage, she complains.

"Walk you home, Marnie?" said Joel.

Susannah grinned at me and faded away. We had an unspoken agreement that if a boy appeared, all else must cease to matter. I waved good-bye to her. "What happened to your game, Joel?" I said.

"The other team's gym has a serious leak in the roof and we couldn't transfer the game to our high school because there's a gymnastics meet scheduled there, so I've got the afternoon off."

I decided to ask Joel in to our apartment. Mother had made a carrot cake a few days ago and carrot cakes were yummy and kept well. *Marnie, help me cook . . . I'm in a hurry, Mother . . . We need to talk, Marnie . . . Here, I'll grate the carrots for you, did I tell you I'm in charge of the French class banquet and Susannah and I made semi-final tryouts in cheerleading and we have a special rehearsal for the spring concert . . . ? That's wonderful, Marnie, but . . . Bye, Mother!*

I thought, I really must make time to talk to Mother one of these days. Then I thought, Joel and I can sit on the loveseat and eat cake. It must be called a loveseat for a reason. Maybe we'll kiss. A real grown-up kiss.

When I was very small my favorite picture book involved a little boy who detested toy tools that broke and pretend toys that weren't real. What he wanted was a real shovel to dig a real hole, the biggest hole in the world. Well, I never wanted a shovel or dirt, but I always wanted real grown-up things. Like kisses.

Every time I went to a junior high dance, afterward the boy would look at me very nervously, and we would kind of leap at each other, lips first. We pretended those were kisses. We both knew kisses had better be better than that, or the heck with the whole thing.

". . . some chestnuts, Marnie?"

That would teach me to daydream. "Oh, Joel, that's nice of you. But I've got some homemade cake at home. How about that instead?"

"Sounds good. You like cooking?"

"Actually I don't know anything about cooking. Mother assigns me the chopping or the scraping or the peeling, but she's the one who actually cooks."

"You're lucky. I have to clean up. My mother says she's not raising any male chauvinist pig, so I scour pots and mop floors and do laundry and scrub the oven."

"How horrible. The only thing I ever do is make my bed. What's your attitude after all that housekeeping? Are you a male chauvinist?"

"I am someone who definitely plans to earn enough money to hire somebody to clean for me."

"What do you want to do, anyhow?"

"I have no idea. It really worries me, Marnie. A person should at least have some faint remote glimmer of his future by the time he's eighteen, but I don't."

I poked the up button for the elevator to our apartment.

"You know what?" I confided to Joel. "Every time I ride in an elevator, I wonder what I should do if the cable breaks. Should I be calm and stoic, accepting my squashed fate, holding the elbows of old ladies and speaking gently to little children? Or should I leap up and down, trying to be on an up jump when the elevator whacks the bottom?"

Joel howled with laughter. "I vote for being on an up jump," he said, and immediately began leaping up and down. Basketball players tend to be good leapers.

"Stop it!" I said. "What if the elevator stops

and somebody sees you leaping all over the place like Super Frog?"

He leaped harder.

"You're going to break the cable just jumping," I protested.

But he kept jumping, and when the doors opened at our floor one of our neighbors was standing there, looking at Joel as if he were a disease she thought the World Health Organization had eradicated. I blushed nine shades of red, but Joel simply bowed to her and swept me out of the elevator to our door. Oh, to be a senior and not blush!

"Mother?" I yelled, unlocking the door. But nobody was home. I was delighted. I am fond of my parents, but conversation that is interesting and funny when I'm alone with another kid is stilted and difficult when my folks are around. I'm not sure why. Mother is polite, but no matter who is with me — even Susannah — I always feel she wishes I had found somebody better.

"So. What's to eat?" said Joel.

"There are quite a few choices, but you're not going to like most of them any more than you did last time. Mother is still deep into her natural foods kick."

"That carrot juice she foisted off on me last week was nauseating."

"Well, today we're featuring pomegranate juice, iced herb tea, buttermilk, carrot cake made with whole wheat and pineapple, and four varieties of tasty cheese."

"Carrot cake? Cake made with carrots? I thought you meant real cake, not rabbit food."

"Actually carrot cake is moist and good and you don't even know the carrots are there."

"Then why add them?" Scowling, Joel broke off a corner of cake. "Hey. It *is* good. Okay. I'll have carrot cake and . . . and . . . and ice water."

We took our food into the living room to eat.

I love our living room. I never want to move or change a thing, because it is perfect. My mother has bought every interior decorating magazine ever printed and she has a wonderful color sense, anyway. The walls are a warm, welcoming yellow, not blatty gold or pumpkiny orange or little girl weak, but a cozy, rich yellow. Lots of cherry and walnut furniture with neutral upholstery and pillows and a forest of green plants on the south window ledge. An oil painting my parents got for an investment splashes a sort of half-eaten rainbow over the dining table. Everywhere are magazines, books, and lovely pieces of pottery. People who visit us invariably exclaim that ours is the handsomest, homiest room they've ever seen. "Like the country," they say happily, as if a room that was "like the city" wouldn't be half so nice.

"You have to take lots of vitamins and pills with this natural diet, Marnie?"

"Oh, no, absolutely not. Mother believes an honest diet from wholesome foods supplies you with every nutrient you need."

"I saw you getting a candy bar from the vending machine."

"I know. I sin. Mother wouldn't be pleased. She thinks she's taught me enough about the evils of refined sugar and artificial additives that I'll make informed choices. And I do."

Joel grinned. "When you eat junk, at least you know it's junk, huh?" He got himself another piece of cake and began leafing through the magazines that filled an enormous brass bucket by Mother's painstakingly constructed false fireplace. "Strange stuff," he commented. *Organic Gardening. The Mother Earth News. Dairy Goat Journal. Alternative Energy Sourcebook. Country Living.* "Hmmm. Do I want to learn how to make my compost quicker and better?"

I tried to laugh, but a quiver of Lucas-induced fear was darting around in my brain. What had happened to *House Beautiful* and *Fortune* and *Glamour?*

"Catnip as a cash crop," read Joel. "Say. I've been worried about my college major, but with this article I can get my whole future squared away."

"And look over here," I said. "How to grind your own bread flour. How to make windchimes out of discarded Coke bottle bottoms. How to tighten a fence."

"Tighten a fence," said Joel. "Who would have thought that fences had to be tightened?" He stared at a photo of an apparently self-sufficient couple posed, beaming, in front of a shack in which they actually lived. They wore shapeless bib overalls and were knee deep in huge overgrown leaves that looked like a vegetable's nightmare and turned out to be rhubarb. "I can't even stand the thought of gardening," said Joel. "All those bugs and worms, sinking up to my ankles in dirt. That field trip today was enough country to last me for years."

I fought my fears, telling myself Lucas was a fool and a creep and nothing he ever said was worth two cents, but I was suddenly aware that in the last year there had been an awful lot of changes in our household.

"Look at these classified ads," exclaimed Joel. " 'Sincere, virile, outdoor-type philosopher looking for willing companion interested in sunshine, common sense, holistic living, and pigs to help run my farm in the Ozarks.' " Joel choked on his carrot cake. "Don't know why the man specifies common sense. It's a cinch he's not offering any."

I was seeing my mother reading seed catalogs the way she used to read *Redbook*. My father thumbing through the farm and ranch edition of the Sears catalog looking at beehive equipment. The library books, not mysteries or spy novels these days, but *How to Raise Chickens and Ducks, How to Buy Country Property, Your Best Woodstove Buy*.

Both my parents would read anything. From the ingredients on the Cheerios box to forty-five things to do with Arm & Hammer Baking Soda. From coffee table photograph collections of Andes Mountains civilizations to guides for getting ham radio licenses.

So they were reading about farming now. So

what? It was just this year's winter entertainment. That was all.

"Enough of this rural stuff," said Joel, a sentiment with which I heartily agreed. "Back to what matters. There's a new Burt Reynolds movie playing at that theater down by the school. You want to go tonight after supper?"

He had asked me. A really truly date with Joel Fiori. I couldn't wait to telephone Susannah. And what should I wear? What would . . . "I'd love to, Joel," I said. We leaned toward each other just a fraction, kind of apprehensively, but very eagerly, and I thought, Do I want my first real grown-up kiss to be with my eyes closed, or —

"Yoo hoo, I'm home!" shouted my mother.

Joel leaned back and turned the page in the magazine. Thus went my first grown-up kiss.

"Hello, Marnie. Hello, Joel. How are you?" She didn't wait for an answer, but bustled on into the kitchen to put down her packages.

"Mother, Joel and I are going to the movies tonight after supper, okay?" I knew it would be okay. Susannah and I go out by ourselves lots of times and Mother never objects. And with Joel!

But Mother appeared in the kitchen door and said no. She actually said no. An expression of disgust fleetingly crossed Joel's face, as if I had lied to him about my age, and he hadn't realized I was going to turn out to be some little girl.

"But, Mother — "

"I'm sorry, Marnie. I didn't know you were making plans or I'd've told you not to. Today we found out — well, things have rapidly come to a

26   .

head, Marnie, and tonight we have something to talk about."

"We can talk over supper," I offered, "or when I get back from the movies."

"No, Marnie. You wouldn't listen then."

Joel was trying to look as if he were a passing traveling salesman. He got up and his whole body took on a leaving-now look.

"Marnie," said my mother, "all you do is whip from one thing to another. This is serious and you have to sit still and give it the amount of time it deserves. The Petersons are coming over for dinner to talk about it with us and you are not going anywhere."

I felt slapped. Right in front of Joel.

"Joel, I'm afraid I have some chores for Marnie to get to. Nice to see you." She literally escorted him to the door. I couldn't believe it! Not even allowing Joel a moment to say good-bye. She was acting as if Joel were a dust kitten she needed to sweep out.

"See you, Marnie," said Joel, and he left quickly, shutting the door behind him.

"Mother, how could you? You were positively rude. What's wrong with seeing a movie with Joel? Joel is a super person. He's very important to me. And just because the Petersons are coming to dinner! Mother, they come all the time." What would Joel say to the senior girl he'd call next to go to that movie with him? *I thought about dating a sophomore girl once, but she had to have her mother's — no, make that Mommy's — no, Mummie's — permission to go anywhere.*

27

I angrily brushed away tears, swallowing a lump in my throat. How could Mother be so thick? So unsympathetic?

She didn't seem to notice my tears or hear my complaints. "Set the table for six, Marnie. Use that beautiful slubbed woven cloth we got from the weaver in Tennessee. And the wooden-handled knives, forks, and spoons."

"But — "

"There isn't time for arguing, Marnie. Set the table."

Maybe because there are just three of us, two grownups and one daughter, we don't have many arguments. We get along. My mother's first rule is, If you can't say something nice, don't say anything at all. Every now and then we have a long silence. Mostly we shrug off the hurts and annoyances and go on being pleasant.

So I didn't have the background to yell at my mother. I'd never done it before.

But then, she'd never thrown out my almost boyfriend before, and refused me my first really truly date.

I would just as soon have smashed the plates as set the table with them. "Mother, what's so important about this dinner?"

The Petersons come over a lot. Mr. Peterson and my father work in the same brokerage firm and Mrs. Peterson and my mother are old sorority sisters who like to have coffee in the mornings and talk about setting up a kitchen enterprise, the way energetic superwomen in the magazines do. But nothing ever came of it.

My mother was a whirlwind in the kitchen, which was very unusual. She likes to cook, and does it slowly and methodically — says it's a deep pleasure and shouldn't be rushed. That night she whipped through the preparation of an involved meal in a fraction of her normal speed. And she wouldn't answer my questions. She wasn't being obstructive: She just seemed to have her mind on fifty other more important things.

Nothing has ever been more important to my mother than me. Yet I had the distinct feeling that I was at the bottom of her thoughts, that she'd brushed me out the way she'd removed Joel.

"Not five plates, Marnie. I said six. Lucas is coming, too."

"Lucas! You know I detest Lucas." It was the ultimate blow! To be forced to exchange an evening with Joel for one with Lucas.

"I know nothing of the sort. I just know that you and Lucas are involved in this."

"Involved in what? Are we all plotting the perfect crime?"

My mother laughed gaily. She took my face in both hands and kissed the top of my nose with a queer tenderness. "No, baby. The perfect life."

Maybe they were arranging a financially intelligent marriage between Lucas and me. One that would produce genetically satisfactory grandchildren for them.

But I was finding it hard to breathe. Goats and strawberries.

Lucas just knows my weak spots, I told myself. He knows that nature is something I detest, so he made that up to shake me.

I set the plates down carefully, because I was still tempted to break them and they were too beautiful. Thick, handmade pottery my mother had acquired on each of the long southern weekends. Lovely, lacy wildflowers had been pressed into the wet clay before baking and glazing, and the plates had an ethereal suggestion of meadows in bloom. If they were mine, I'd keep them on a shelf to look at, but Mother likes to use her good things.

Cork trivets for the casserole in the oven. This was made of soybean mush, fresh tomatoes, peppers, and three cheeses, and it tasted exactly like lasagne, so I always wanted to know why we couldn't just go ahead and have lasagne. Mother would say irritably, "*Mar*nie," as if my name were a nutritional explanation.

I tossed the huge salad: lettuce, sprouts, bits of red cabbage, tomatoes, green peppers, onion, raw cauliflower, and broccoli. I wrapped the whole wheat rolls in the cotton cloth my mother embroidered for wrapping rolls in. ROLLS, it says.

The sight of the embroidery suddenly made me understand something. A pattern to my mother's life.

I don't think I had ever really thought about her life before. I guess I thought that grownups, and my parents in particular, were "done."

Cooked, so to speak.

Isn't the definition of a grownup "finished"? Not dead-type finished, but polished-type finished, as in — well, you know. Done.

Done growing up, done changing, done fretting about "life" or "truth," because you were there. Wherever "there" was.

But Mother never got "there." All that decorating. All that floundering between the perfect houseplant and the perfect club. All those coffee hours talking. All those books about every subject under the sun. All those peculiar skills she would suddenly learn — from Aran-style knitting (I got a gorgeous pullover from that stage), to dying her own wool, to an abortive stab at stained glass window-making. All those causes — everything from Save the Seals to the Bloodmobile, and none of them sticking with her.

She's there, I thought. Whatever is coming tonight is what she really and truly wants.

It was like standing on a cliff, and knowing your mother would pull you right over the edge with her if she thought it was right.

But the doorbell rang, like Mr. Ricks' whistle, and startled me out of my thoughts.

Chapter III

For the very first time in my life, Mr. Peterson did not say hello by telling me he was indubitably honored by reacquainting himself with my charming presence. He actually hugged me. "Hey, girl! Ready to roll?"

Mr. Peterson? Slang? Affection?

Mrs. Peterson hugged me, too, which wasn't unusual, but this time she said absolutely nothing at all (which was impossible, she must have had her larynx removed) and just looked at my mother with glistening eyes.

Lucas slunk in behind them, looking as if he were hostage to a pair of untrustworthy revolutionaries in some disease-ridden hole of a country. "I was in the middle of a good book," he told me, snarling.

He thought *he'd* had to give up something for this dinner!

"They tell you yet?" he said.

Everybody but me knew exactly what was going on. They all looked at me gently, as if I were a sweet, small child who couldn't be expected to understand, but they loved me anyway. "No," I said.

And then my father came bounding in from the office. My father, who usually dragged home, sagged on a chair, to listen to the news with all the enthusiasm of one hearing coffin nails hammered. He picked me up and swung me around the way he used to when I was tiny and liked to hide in the linen closet before bedtime. "We got it, honey, we got it!" he said gleefully. He dropped me, hugged Mother, hugged *each* of the Petersons, including Lucas, who nearly died, and everybody laughed.

Everybody except Lucas and me.

I could not recall having anything in common with Lucas before. "Tell me," I demanded.

"I think we should have our dinner first," said Mother. "When we're relaxed and full and calm, we can talk at our leisure and make things absolutely clear without omissions."

"What a good idea," said Mrs. Peterson, "Now, Marnie, I want you to start calling me Aunt Ellen. And Mr. Peterson Uncle Bob. From now on meals are going to be a family affair and we have to set a precedent, don't we?"

They all giggled again.

The Petersons, giggling. It was one for the books. Elegant, wordy, staid, and giggling.

Lucas played with his casserole. My stomach was knotted so badly I couldn't even eat the hot rolls with sweet butter. ("Margerine," says my mother, "is an unnatural food. We eat what God

33

set on earth for us to eat and our bodies will be healthier for it.")

I know what it is! I thought suddenly, and the mouthful of salad went down after all. We're buying a weekend place in the Smoky Mountains. Probably can't afford it except as a joint expense. "It" must be the special A frame or log cabin they've been yearning for.

A weekend vacation house. I didn't mind that. I might even go once or twice, when I didn't have anything special to do here at home. As long as Susannah could come along, of course. Otherwise, what would there be to do in the country?

And that explained all Mother's excitement: another place to decorate.

I sighed with relief, and then I became aware that the entire table was silent and looking at me again. Even Lucas — with a sort of pity and interest which was a perfectly infuriating combination.

"You're a spinning top, Marnie," said my father gently. "We love you, very very much, but we don't love your frenetic life or your jumble of worthless activities. We feel you've become alienated from the way of life we want you to have."

Worthless activities? Did he mean cheerleading, or special chorus?

"And you, too, Lucas," said my father, facing Lucas, who flushed. "Caught up in all sorts of goals and values that just don't matter. Urban city-type feelings we don't want in our precious children."

34

I set my fork down, little waves of worry breaking over me.

"We've been waiting to hear whether we got the land we wanted. Several other people were bidding on the farm and we couldn't say much until we knew for sure. But today our lawyer called from North Carolina and right now the Petersons and the MacDonalds are the joint owners of a two-hundred acre farm."

For weekends, I told myself. For July.

"For all of our sakes, Marnie, for yours, mine, Ellen's, and Bob's, your mother's, and Lucas's, we're leaving the city. No more rat race. We're going back to the land. The six of us. Together."

Chapter IV

"What do you mean, back to the land?" I said. My tongue felt like soybean mush. A substitute.

"Real honest farming," said Mr. Peterson. Uncle Bob. It was astonishing how his affected vocabulary had dropped from him, as if it had been a disguise no longer needed. "A mule and some goats and a flock of hens for eggs. Our own woods to supply our own firewood. Water from our own springs. Strawberries fresh from our own field. Asparagus rows, orchards, vegetable patches, fields of corn."

"A mule?" I repeated. I don't believe this, I thought. A *mule*? An hysterical giggle began to percolate in my chest. What would I say to Joel, for whom civilization was downtown?

"We've wanted to get out of this life for a long time," said Mrs. Peterson. Aunt Ellen. "But we just couldn't see our way financially."

"But now we've got our land," said my mother

in jubilation, as if her candidate had just won the presidency and inflation would end in sixty minutes. "And we'll be selling the microwave ovens, the televisions, the blenders, the stereo sets. We," she said, and she actually took Aunt Ellen's hand across the table and clasped it tightly, "we are going to be free."

"Free from what?" I said.

"The demands and burdens of city life," said Uncle Bob.

"I told you so," said Lucas.

I hate people who say I told you so. Especially in Lucas' stupid newborn foghorn. "I know a good shrink you could go to," I said to my father. "Psychiatrists are all the rage now. Maybe that's what you need."

He gave me a funny smile. "That's what we'd need if we stayed, Marnie. But we're getting out now. And most of all for your sake."

For my sake?

"Look at Lucas, swept up by the need to score high on college boards, the need to be a National Merit finalist, the need to achieve ninety-five averages in math, the need to win every debate, the need to write term papers that would be acceptable in college. His whole life is a book and a desk. And you, Marnie! Unable to survive without your television comedies. Impossible to live with unless you get your daily overdose of Pepsi or Coke. You can't function without shallow friends babbling on the telephone. Can't appear in school unless you dress in exactly what everyone else has. We have to get you kids away, teach you something of the real, beautiful world, before you're completely corrupted."

If growing up is knowing when not to hit your head on a brick wall, I grew up quite a bit in that moment. I knew there was no use defending my activities, my friends, or my school. And it was definitely not the time to mention my pressing need for rhinestone-studded disco slippers.

I've got to make concessions, I thought desperately. Fast, because they aren't kidding. This is no whim. Not a night course in stained glass ornaments. They mean this.

"I won't watch TV anymore," I said quickly. "It's a good idea for you to sell the television. I should read more. And TV isn't that important. I can understand — "

"Marnie," said my mother, "it's deeper than that."

I knew how the sailors felt when Columbus told them, Oh, by the way, we're planning to sail off the edge. Trust me. The world is round.

Trust them. Farming is fun. You, too, can own a mule.

"I still don't see how you plan to get any money," said Lucas. "I mean, even if everything grows and we raise our own food and heat with our own wood, we'll still need money. We'll have to buy shoes, and pay taxes on the land, and pay for the telephone and the electricity and the diesel fuel for the tractor."

"One cash crop should cover the few needs we'll have, Lucas. As for the telephone and the electricity, we aren't going to have either one. We have bought a small Gravely tractor and a chain saw, but that's about all that will need fuel."

"A chain saw?" I said. "What is that? A medieval instrument of torture? You'll chain us to a saw to make us cut wood?"

They howled with laughter. Good old Marnie, always in there with a one-liner. But nobody explained what a chain saw was.

For some time the adults spoke reverently about "the land." Obviously country land was superior to city land, which lay under cement sidewalks and didn't count. Uncle Bob told us how he had lived a life of quiet desperation, and finally, like Thoreau, had decided to live for truth and beauty.

"But I have an important debate coming up," said Lucas. "And next year is my senior year. I have plans."

"You'll go to school in the country, Lucas. Probably a better system there anyway. But school doesn't really matter. Your real education will be on the land. Coming to grasp nature's plans and your place in them."

Aunt Ellen said, "I've had conferences with your principal. Since you'll be missing the last six weeks of school, you'll be taking final exams week after next and because both of you have good grades, I expect there will be no problem getting credit for the whole year. Now, we won't enroll you in school once we move, because we'll need you working with us to get the farm started up. Next September you'll start locally. But don't worry about it. School isn't a priority."

39

"It is for me," said Lucas.

Uncle Bob put an arm around his son. "This will be good for you, Lucas. I know you think you'll miss something. But take my word for it. As a brilliant writer once said, 'The reason they're called lessons is, they lessen from day to day.' "

I thought about that. "What brilliant writer?" I said suspiciously.

"Lewis Carroll. In *Alice in Wonderland*."

"That seems suitable," I said. If anything had gone mixed-up, inside-out, and topsy-turvy, it was our lives, right this minute.

"Just think," said my mother dreamily. "Walking on thick green grass. Over our own meadows, along pine-needle paths in deep woods."

"There's more to farming than poetry," said Lucas. "There's manure, drought, crop failure, poor soil, insect attacks or blight, and — "

"And we'll learn how to handle that sort of thing together," said his father.

"What am I supposed to tell people at school?" I demanded. I could just see myself going up to Joel and Susannah and Eve and Kay and all Joel's senior teammates and telling them I was off to the southern mountains with Lucas Peterson, a mule, and lots of good honest dirt.

"Tell them you're going to be free," said my mother.

Lucas began to laugh. Obviously the thought of Marnie MacDonald telling Joel Fiori's crowd that she was going to be free at last made his evening much better.

40

"Free," I said. "If I were free I'd make a different choice." And then I thought of Susannah. "Mother, I could stay with Susannah. Her parents wouldn't mind."

"Marnie, it is one thing to spend a weekend now and then with a friend. I assure you that her parents would not take on another child for several years. You are only fifteen. Anyway, the whole point of this is to get you away from here as well as us."

"Isn't it surprising?" said Aunt Ellen. "They're so young. I would have thought the young could understand change better. Embrace change just for the sake of change."

"The young," said Uncle Bob, "often cling to familiarity."

"The young," said Aunt Ellen, "often — "

"Will you stop calling us the young?" said Lucas. "We are not a litter of something."

"I want to know why you didn't tell me?" I said. "Fifteen is old enough to be told about volcanic eruptions in one's family. Fifteen is even old enough to be consulted."

"We tried, Marnie. You wouldn't listen. You kept rushing around, refusing to take the time to hear what we had to say. Frantically going from one thing to another in your empty life."

"Empty! My life is crammed. And I have so much more to do here. I don't want to leave school, I don't want to do this!"

"We know what is best, Marnie. Moving to the country will be a blessing for you."

"A blessing! What am I supposed to do? Rejoice in the raising of lima beans? Thrill to the odor of manure on my shoe? Sing with joy at the prospect of pruning a tree?"

I had hurt them. Deflated them like balloons. They sagged, the exhilaration gone. They looked older, and less ready to go on a vacation.

I felt like a monster. I found myself wanting to apologize. But they were the rotten ones! But I had never, not purposely at least, been unpleasant to my parents. The hurt look on my mother's face whipped me.

"Well, I," said Lucas, "I, personally, am not going."

"Nonsense," said his father.

And Aunt Ellen produced a notebook and they began to compose the newspaper ad for the yard sale at which we would sell everything we owned.

42

Chapter V

By lunch Monday the entire high school knew about it. I was the most popular girl in school, and mostly with the boys. It seemed so unfair. After all these years of wanting to attract them by my scintillating conversation, my sleek gleaming hair, my flawless makeup, they came in droves to hear how I was going to dig my own well.

"Now, how will you do field work?" said our best tennis player. "Horse, mule, or tractor?"

"Tractor. We don't really want to spade up fifty acres by hand." I was quoting. I had been told that we must keep a united front and I must not tell people I was being dragged along.

"Is it true you won't have electricity?" said the student government president, whose policy was never to look at sophomores. Diego was unbelievably handsome. He sat down beside me, squashing between me and Susannah. Susannah loved it. I had mixed feelings. "Yes, we're selling every appliance that uses electricity. No, we're not going to generate electricity by wind or solar power as far as I know."

A lot of the boys thought I was lucky. "I wish I could go," they said. I wished it, too.

But most people were not envious. "Your folks are flaky," said Kay flatly.

I had made a promise. But it was the final insult to have to defend my parents when I too thought they were flaky. "No," I said, "just different." I tried to imply that Kay's boring family would never do anything exciting like this. Then I thought, Oh, to be in a boring family like Kay's!

"And Lucas Peterson is doing this with you?" said the squash team champion. "I didn't know Lucas ever had any exercise beyond turning the page in his library book. He's going to split firewood, sink fenceposts, dig gardens, build henhouses, and fix generators?"

"Mercy!" said Eve. "Are you going to do all that, Marnie?"

It had a familiar ring to it.

"But that's horrible," said Anne. "They can't tear you away from civilization like that, can they? Especially with a wimp like Lucas."

"Lucas isn't wimpy," I said, and I could have bitten off my tongue. Lucas wasn't my family, no matter what Mother and Dad claimed about togetherness. I didn't have to defend *him*.

"Just the word farm makes me shudder," said Susannah. "Getting up at four in the morning, milking cows covered with flies."

"Goats," said Kay, "they're keeping goats."

Everybody began to snicker. I wasn't Marnie MacDonald anymore. I was a weird kid whose weird parents were going to raise goats.

"But how can you function without electricity?" said the student government president. "Wash your clothes on a rock in a river? Heat your bath water on a stove? Run that stove on wood?"

Just the sentences made my knees weak. And I had a sneaking suspicion nobody was going to hire a maid to do any of that, either.

"Gosh," said Kay. "In winter it'll be dark by four o'clock and you won't have any lights. I guess you can play Abe Lincoln. Dip candles and wear hoop skirts."

"Abe Lincoln," said Lucas, materializing from nowhere, "hardly ever wore a hoop skirt. Come on, Marnie." He took my arm and hauled me out of the cafeteria.

"What do you think you're doing?" I said through my teeth. "You're not a shepherd yet, Lucas Peterson, and I'm not your sheep. Stop leading me."

"They were laughing at us," said Lucas. "And I won't have it."

We sat on the granite steps of the courtyard entrance. The sun was warm and yellow, but it failed to make me feel good. I felt like a storm — wild and black and angry.

"It's the end of my life," said Lucas.

But then I couldn't stoop to agreeing with Lucas, either. "Oh, don't be so melodramatic,"

I snapped. "We're just moving. Millions of families move every year."

"You sure changed sides in a hurry."

"So I won't be on the same side as you." I could just see Lucas, when wood-splitting time had come, retreating to a cozy corner to write haiku about the joys of pastoral living.

Lucas regarded me as if I were an ice cream cone he'd dropped in the gutter and been forced to eat anyway. "This is going to be the longest year of my life."

"Year?" I grabbed him. "Have they decided to do it for just one year? Oh, Lucas, I can endure anything for a year. Even you. Really and truly, and then we'll come home again?"

He extricated himself fastidiously from my fingers. "No, Marnie. They're going for good. It isn't a whim or a hobby. But I'm going on to college, no matter what happens. *Nothing* is going to keep me from *my* goals."

For a moment I almost wanted to know what these goals were he so passionately wanted to achieve. Most of the boys I'd ever talked to were like Joel, completely at sea, no idea what they wanted. Then I remembered this was elbow-kneed, wimpy Lucas. "You got your braces off," I said.

"Yeah. This morning. Turns out orthodontist bills are one of the things we aren't taking with us."

He looked different with white teeth. "Smile, Lucas."

"Marnie, I'm not your boyfriend. Save the flirting for Joel."

"Flirting! With *you?* Why, you — "

And then he did smile, proud of getting a rise out of me. And he had a beautiful smile; not at all the sort of smile you would expect a Lucas to have.

Between classes, Joel bought me a candy bar from the vending machine in the lobby. I thought, Not only will I never see Joel again, I'll probably never see a vending machine again.

It was impossible to explain Joel, and all that he had stood for, to my parents. Impossible to explain why I was crying and what they expected me to give up so easily.

"You are mourning for a vending machine?" yelled my father. "Marnie, weep for children starving in Cambodia, weep for Jews persecuted in Russia, but for God's sake, don't weep over a vending machine."

"You know what I keep thinking?" said Susannah.

"No, what?"

"Dating is sort of a ladder. And you were up quite a ways. And Joel should have been one of your steps. Next year when he's at college you should be on a different step. But your parents have knocked you right off the whole ladder."

"From now on there's no one but Lucas," I said glumly.

47

"Maybe he'll grow on you."

"What, like some insidious cancer?" Neither of us knew whether to laugh or cry.

My parents' friends and acquaintances were astonishingly envious. (Except for the ones who figured we had an infectious disease and kept away.) They'd come over to talk longingly of having a raspberry patch and a few hens for fresh eggs. "Pretty exciting, huh, Marnie?" said the senior vice president of Dad's old brokerage firm.

My longings were confined to escalators leading to the jewelry department, disco dances with glittering lights, and the senior prom to which Joel would never ask me because I would be gone. "No, it's awful."

"You're a city girl, are you?"

"A happy city girl."

"Well, hang in there, Marnie. You'll have Lucas for company. That'll help a lot."

He was serious.

I went to the movies with Joel after all. And once, roller skating. It was fun, but not much. It bore too much resemblance to the last meal before the execution. Still, it was nifty to have a handsome, strong boy like Joel squiring me around so much.

The days passed with terrifying speed. There was no time to worry about the finals: I just took them, with Lucas at a desk in the same room taking his finals; and we both did okay. Not fine, but okay.

I tried arguing with my parents. "Doesn't work, does it?" said Lucas mournfully. "They pay about as much attention to me as if I were lecturing on theories of economic controls for the Rumanian peasant."

Besides, our parents were so happy. There is something unapproachable about total happiness. It seems sinful to kick it.

Every night either we would go to the Petersons or they would come to our apartment, and Lucas and I would read up on bee-keeping, or wide row vegetable planting, or the art of building a stone wall. I found I had a sixth sense to tell me when Lucas was going to roll his eyes: I'd roll my own back and somehow we'd hang onto the shreds of sanity.

I got to keep my bed, my blankets, quilts, and designer sheets, the clothes my mother deemed suitable (the ugly, sturdy ones), and whatever else would fit into my chest. That chest was our best antique: a pre-Revolutionary six-board blanket chest my great-grandmother got at an auction some sixty years ago. It's beautiful, but it doesn't hold much. When I put in my old gray wool Eeyore, the stack of chorus programs beginning with the Christmas one in third grade when I fell off the risers, the old plastic doll I washed in the tub with me every night right up to junior high, my journals and diaries (I tended to make six entries and forget it), my photograph album, and my piggy bank from a kindergarten birthday party, there was hardly room for the add-a-bead necklace that all my friends got together to buy for me.

Everything else in my fifteen-by-fourteen bedroom, with its two walk-in closets, its matching bureaus, and its nine shelves, had to go to the yard sale. Susannah and I spent hours combing through, deciding what to keep. Susannah loved it. She got more treasures than the last two Christmases combined.

I felt cut.

Aunt Ellen celebrated the last meal she'd make in their apartment by cooking homemade old-fashioned gingerbread with whipped cream.

"I wish you two would be more responsive to all we're doing for you," she said, dusting her hands on her big white canvas apron. She was sewing a matching one for me.

"But," said Lucas, and he stopped.

"I know what you mean," I said to him. "There are so many buts it's impossible to choose one and get started on it."

"Have you two declared a truce?" said Aunt Ellen.

"Beggars can't be choosers," said Lucas. I threw my gingerbread at him and got him right in the face.

"Mother, I have to be allowed to take more with me."

"No room, dear. We'll have five rooms. Your father and I'll have one bedroom, The Petersons another, Lucas will share the third bedroom with the pantry shelves we'll build to store all our home-canned produce, and you'll have this dear little loft over the living room. Marnie, you'll be so cozy in winter, as the heat rises from the woodstove. It's going to be so lovely."

"I said, can I take more with me?"

"No, dear, we'll be too cramped for space. Now, what do you think we can get for these two electronic games of yours? And this stack of your records, are they worth anything?"

Aunt Ellen's neighbor's friends had a house in the suburbs with a big yard and good traffic, so we hauled everything over there to tag and sell. The lamps, blender, rotisserie, waffle iron, stereo, crystal, Ping-Pong table, bridge table, five window air conditioners, about a million books (Lucas was in pain over the sale of each one of these), all my old stuffed dolls and toys, Aunt Ellen's electric towel-drying rack, my father's hair dryer, Uncle Bob's electric typewriter, Mother's Cuisinart.

"This is not a joke, then," said Susannah. "I've kept hoping somehow it would turn out to be a joke. After all, this is April first."

"No, it doesn't seem to be a joke," I said. We cried a little. It wouldn't make my mascara run because I wasn't wearing any. Mother threw out my makeup. From now on, she explained, your sparkle will be your own personality. Does it matter, I said, that my eyebrows are blonde and I have only seven visible lashes per lid?

She laughed joyously. She *knew* I would love this "land" of hers once I got there.

My father tied down the last box, wrapped the last old rug around an exposed table corner, and locked the door of the rented moving van. "Let's roll," he cried gaily. My mother and father and Aunt Ellen and Uncle Bob and scores of their friends hugged each other with wild abandon — a phrase from some poem I once had to read in English. I hugged back to prevent a lecture on my shallow vending-machine values. Lucas looked as if he were having a wisdom tooth removed by a garage mechanic.

"Good-bye," said Joel uncertainly. We both blushed. A kiss was impossible with laughing grownups watching.

"Good-bye," I said, my well-rehearsed speech vanishing, replaced by a film of tears.

"Well, son, you want first turn at driving?" said Uncle Bob.

"No," said Lucas curtly. I had never seen him without books before. I wondered what Lucas had been allowed to keep. What they had made him give up.

"Good-bye," cried Susannah, hugging me.

The men got into the moving van, and we women squeezed into the Petersons' old Volkswagen bus, jammed with cartons and trunks, and we were off, clad in blue jeans and hope, for the good life on a farm in North Carolina.

Chapter VI

It was spring when we got to the farm that had been bought without my knowledge or my consent. A scrawny tree resembling a woody weed dotted the woods with lavender ribbons. Wild dogwood frothed pink and white in the pines, and in the field, daisies, black-eyed Susans, and all the members of their tribe waved in the wind. The hills were like green goose pimples on a giant's skin: odd rounded bumps, covered with rough pasture and an occasional gnarled tree.

I was not prepared for North Carolina to be beautiful. I hated the place for not being dreary and dark, like my thoughts.

The little village where we would shop had only a handful of stores. Even the Sears Roebuck store had nothing in it but catalogs to order from. The largest stores were the tractor dealership and FCX. Farmers' Cooperative Exchange, said my mother knowledgeably and happily.

The only thing I wanted to exchange was my life.

Off the main street was a rather small brick building with a sign in front that said, Valley Consolidated High School. The bevy of yellow school buses behind it made me ache for school. For *my* school, where Joel and Susannah and special chorus and the cheerleading team were going right on without me.

Our farmland consisted of two bumping hills sprinkled with apple trees, which had just come into blossoms so beautiful it hurt my throat to see them. "Like bridal lace," said Aunt Ellen, and she was right, but that made me think of falling off Susannah's dating ladder, which made me angry again.

Our home was seven miles from the village. On our narrow, long lane were two other houses. I wondered where the schoolbus would pick up next fall. If the other houses had teenagers in them. If they spoke English.

"This is not Tibet, Marnie," said my mother irritably.

Lucas and I stood staring at what was to be our home while the adults peppered us with superlatives describing the place. "The previous owners thought the orchards were too much hard work," said Uncle Bob, "and they left for the city and factory jobs."

"More misguided souls," said my mother.

"Smart as whips," muttered Lucas.

The house was an old frame building with front porch, side porch, and back porch. From the front you could look out over our little valley, gaze up the rounded hill in front of us, and see beyond it, smoky and blue, the distant mountains of the Ridge. From the back, a huge garden space sprawled in weedy abandon. The side was enclosed by a thick, dense screen of white, blooming shrubs.

I didn't want to look at mountains or shrubs or weeds. I wanted to use my binoculars out the east window of my eleventh floor and watch the construction of the high-rise parking lot going up where an old hotel had been.

We went into the house. I began to see more clearly why the previous owners had left for better surroundings. There was nothing indoors that was not going to require scouring, sanding, painting, or staining.

"Mother," I said, after a complete tour, during which I opened every single door and cupboard.

"Yes, dear?"

"Where is the bathroom?"

There was a pause. She seemed to deliberate how to answer that.

"Uh oh," said Lucas.

"I guess I forgot to mention it, Marnie," said my mother, "but this house doesn't have indoor plumbing."

"I think this *is* Tibet," said Lucas.

"Do you mean to tell me this house doesn't have a bathroom?" I shrieked. After two solid days of driving, when all I wanted was a tiled bath and a long soaking tub or a good hot shower and some nice humid privacy where I could cry in peace — and there was no bathroom?

Lucas and I located the outhouse without

difficulty. It looked just the way they do in cartoons. "Another field trip," said Lucas.

"The first of many, I'm afraid," I said. "Lucas, I can't believe this."

There was no question of whether to laugh or cry. Crying won very easily.

Sitting on the side porch was a pile of split wood. Uncle Bob lit a fire in the huge black wood stove in the kitchen and hauled buckets of water from the well pump to heat up in an enormous bucket on the stove. "In summer," said my father, "we'll rig up an outdoor shower. Gravity will be enough to make the shower work from the spring up on the hill, and the sun's heat will warm it up right through a rubber hose."

"For now?" I said.

"For now, we sponge off."

So we had a women's bathtime and a men's bathtime. There wasn't enough water to hide my weeping.

"This is fun, Marnie," said my mother and Aunt Ellen together.

"This is insane," I said.

Our parents were on a high that never touched Lucas or me. In the other world my only chore had been making my bed, if I felt like it. Now the chores never ended. I lay like glue on the mattress, while the adults leaped up at dawn — yes, dawn — full of verve and energy and even joy.

The vegetable garden was a staggering chore. Although we tilled it with the tractor (Uncle Bob turned out to know all about driving tractors and even all about fixing tractors, which was particularly good, since our twelfth-hand wreck broke down regularly), we had to hand-rake the entire two-acre garden until it satisfied the grown-ups as to tilth and texture. Then we planted about fifty things at intervals so we'd have harvest all summer and fall instead of everything coming ripe at one time. Seeds are very small. You have to plant them one at a time. Stooping.

And in my case, you have to do this with Lucas. Once we had an actual conversation in which we talked about sabotaging the garden. But we decided that wouldn't get us back to the city. We'd just have to live here and starve, instead of live here and eat.

The asparagus trench was probably the worst chore of the summer. This had to be dug, with shovels, eighteen inches deep. Eighteen inches doesn't sound like much until you have to lift it up on the end of your shovel. Furthermore you're supposed to backfill half of that with rotted manure. We obtained the manure from our nearest neighbor, Mr. Shields, who was a very nice man who nevertheless had a small mountain of horse manure he'd been shoveling out of his stable for years. We forked this up on a flat trailer we pulled behind the tractor, and it took one load of manure for the asparagus trench and eleven loads for the rest of the garden. If anybody had told me I'd be shoveling manure instead of dating Joel or experimenting with eye shadow . . . !

"And I don't even like asparagus," said Lucas. "It's slimy and green. It looks like congealed scum from a pond."

"Look at that," I said.

We stood there like convicts on a road gang. Through the meadow on the hillside, our parents ran up to the orchards, laughing, kissing, and actually singing from pure pleasure. "Morning has broken," they sang, "like the first morning. Blackbird is singing, like the first dawn."

According to my father's manuals, wood for heating homes had to be cut at least six months before burning, so it would season, or dry out. We took to our woodlots, cutting down only the dead trees, using the chain saw to remove their branches and cut everything into usable lengths. The chain saw was a wonderful thing, fast and efficient, and it made a noise like a convention of dentists' drills. I hated that sound so much I would turn my back to the others and scream at the top of my lungs when it was going. Nobody noticed and it made me feel a little better.

Then came splitting the wood. Lucas, Dad, and Uncle Bob tried this with the axe and after that, as Lucas said rather grimly, they all had a lot more respect for Abe Lincoln. Then they tried using wedges and a sledge hammer. After one weekend of that, we had about ten logs split and a lot of blisters to treat.

"Got a hydraulic log splitter you could rent," said Mr. Shields, grinning. He often dropped by in late afternoon, for laughs, probably. My parents never seemed to mind how inept or confused or clumsy they were. They'd earnestly ask what to try next, and even take notes on what he said.

I hated not knowing how to do things.

I felt like such a baby, being assigned something, and then not having the remotest idea how to go about doing it.

Lucas learned techniques with a sort of grim determination, as if this were war, and as long as you had to fight, you might as well win. I never heard him complain, though possibly that was because my own complaints drowned his out.

Lucas and I had the dubious honor of being in charge of our flock of chickens. Mr. Shields sold us a dozen eight-week-old pullets and let us dismantle an old hen coop of his and haul it over to our place to rebuild, paint, and fence in. The chickens were surprisingly cute and I actually enjoyed feeding them. It took me one minute to scatter the feed and fourteen minutes to watch the chickens eat, so I told everybody it was a fifteen-minute chore and no one questioned me.

The trouble with these cute, pecking chickens was you had to clean up their droppings every day. And add them to the compost pile — or mountain — Lucas and I were also in charge of.

One way or another, I saw as much of Lucas as I did of dirt, bugs, and outhouses.

At least the amount of work cut down on my homesickness. There was no time to bring out my grief and mull it over. Even at night, a time I always used to reserve for curling up into a little ball and running my mind over my problems, the only thing I had time for was sleep.

I did love my loft bedroom, though. Part of the

attic had been ripped out when the black stove-pipe for the living room's Fisher stove was run up to the roof. The part that was left — barely eleven feet by five feet — was shored up by two posts and railed with one thick beam.

Built flush with the inner wall and the rest of the attic were built-in drawers and a closet. There was space, then, for my mattress, my hope chest, and me. In summer the loft was gaspingly hot, but in winter I found that the heat rose, making it delightfully cozy.

When I wasn't destroying underburrs, tending chickens, figuring out how to milk a goat, shelling peas, chasing the goat when she got away, leaning on my shovel, puffing, or fixing holes in the goat's fence, I was in the kitchen.

We ate at least four times as much as when we didn't work outdoors. It was nothing for the six of us to go through four loaves of homemade bread in a day or polish off a pie at lunch and two bread puddings at supper. I became the bread baker. This meant mixing and kneading and then leaving the kitchen for other chores during the first rising. Then I'd scrub off the accumulated dirt from that chore, punch the dough down to rise again, and go off to rake out the chicken coop, or something equally charming. An hour later, scrub again, form the dough into loaves. More yard work. Scrub. Put loaves in oven. Stand there checking our erratic wood stove for fire, heat, wood, and so on. Take the loaves out to cool

60

and have Lucas literally take an entire loaf with him to eat while he was driving the tractor among the apple trees, dragging the mower after him to cut the tall meadow grass. It was a sweet-smelling job, where you got to sit down, and I envied Lucas, although I didn't envy the terrible burn he got once. The loaves weren't even done when it was time to bake more. I knew Lucas was hungry, and I knew the reason I'd baked was for people to eat, but I couldn't stand to see anybody eat my bread, because all it meant to me was having to bake more.

And, of course, there was laundry. We had an old washer that you handpumped to make the clothes and suds churn. We had to haul the water and heat it on the woodstove to get it hot enough to melt the soap. "Please, please, please, let's just drive to a laundromat," I said. But Mother and Aunt Ellen actually loved the laundry that way.

We got mail, which did not make up for the fact that we had no telephone, and the mail itself was as depressing as no telephone.

Joel wrote exactly once, four lines scrawled on a postcard to say he'd been accepted at NYU and would major in accounting. It sounded like such an urban thing to do. I could just see him in a vested suit, pinstriped and citified. And here I was in bibbed overalls.

Susannah wrote weekly at first, and then her letters came less and less often. She had begun dating a friend of Joel's. "And I have you to thank for it," she wrote, describing her social whirl. "If I hadn't been sitting next to you during all that commotion about you going farming, Pete would never have noticed me." Joel, she wrote, took a girl named Victoria to the senior prom. Somebody from parochial school. Three juniors made the cheerleading team. Susannah wasn't one but she didn't mind, Pete was keeping her busy. They had gone to three movies. Had I seen any of them? I must not miss the super thriller about the almost nuclear explosion. How many cute boys had I met so far? Was farming fun? Susannah bet we had lots of fresh tomatoes. No more time to write, she was off to tennis camp.

"One thing for sure," I said to my mother. "I'd play a mean game of tennis now. Look at my muscles."

"Another thing for sure," she said, reading Susannah's latest letter, "she's right about having lots of fresh tomatoes."

Gardens, especially your first garden, are supposed to include a few failures. At least something is supposed to have the decency not to grow.

Not our garden.

Everything grew.

And grew, and grew, and grew.

We had millions of beans to snap and billions of tomatoes to can. If we'd had electricity, we could've dropped everything into plastic bags and thrown them into a freezer, but we had to can everything to have food for the winter.

Canning is horrid.

First you dip the tomatoes in boiling water (on top of your fired-up woodstove) and slide off the peel. Then (it's August and ninety degrees outdoors and probably a hundred twenty in the kitchen) you core the tomatoes, force them through the strainer, and pour the juice into Mason jars. Aunt Ellen puts these in the pressure canner also on top of your woodstove and the three of you stand there gasping for breath, fanning yourselves, trying not to burn each other on hot Mason jars.

While I panted, Mother and Aunt Ellen chattered about things like goat milk. They had figured out how to make one soft and one not-so-soft cheese, but they had not managed to make a decent goat butter.

"We need a cow," said Uncle Bob, coming in for a glass of goat milk.

"We need a cow," said Lucas, getting himself tomato juice, "like we need a hole in the head."

I was very glad to see the tomato juice go anywhere other than a jar I had to boil and seal. "Holes in the head," I told him, "are what we have most of around here."

"Marnie, I am not amused," said my mother.

The men went back out. Sweeping the floor I found a letter to Lucas from one of his friends back home. Temptation overcame me and I read it. The debate team, said his friend, had won the regional championship, without Lucas, obviously. So much for Lucas and me being necessary back home. He'd been as easily replaced as I'd been by this Victoria, may she rest with nightmares.

I wondered vaguely how much Lucas hurt over that. I'd never know. Lucas never told anybody anything, and least of all me. He just worked, and ate, and worked some more. He came back a few hours and a million tomatoes later for another drink. "Having fun, girls?" he said.

"Oh, yes!" cried our mothers, actually meaning it.

"Oh, yes," I said sarcastically.

"For laughs, Marnie," said Lucas, "come on out back and help me. The old outhouse hole is full. I just covered it and now I'm digging another hole."

I decided canning wasn't so bad.

"We're out of canning jar rings, salt, sugar, and a few other things," said Aunt Ellen. "Lucas, would you mind very much going into town and getting them?"

Lucas allowed as how he wouldn't mind too much. "Would I mind?" he said reverently. "No, ma'am, I wouldn't, I'm going, I'm leaving, it's no problem whatsoever."

"I need to go, too," I said quickly. "Lucas wouldn't know a jar ring if he tripped over it." Considering that Lucas had indeed tripped over jar rings, and even bought them before, that was a statement full of loopholes, but our mothers overlooked this and said I could go along. "Wait till I change, Lucas," I said.

"Wait till *you* change?" he replied. "I'm the one who was digging a latrine."

So we both changed and got into the old VW

bus to drive into the village. We were so excited you'd have thought we had tickets to the Bolshoi Ballet. We got groceries, picked up the jar rings, got goat feed at FCX, and sunglasses for Lucas at the tiny "department" store (if it had any departments, they weren't visible), and then we walked around the village. There wasn't much to it. To our city-starved eyes the whole town wasn't much more than a single block. There wasn't even a traffic light, let alone traffic.

We arrived at the school, which had a hot, blank look, the look of all schools closed up for August. Valley Consolidated High School. It didn't look promising, but it would undoubtedly beat subsistence farming.

"Next week," said Lucas. He sighed.

Seven more days, I thought. "Do you think it'll be any good?"

"If you can believe it from a bookworm, Marnie, I don't even care. I'm just so eager to get away from the manure piles, the orchards, and the wood that needs splitting, it can be the lousiest school in the U.S.A. and I'll love it."

I laughed. It wasn't a sound I'd made much that summer. "I used to think of school as a place where I had to work, work, work all the time. Now I'm looking forward to school as a place to escape work, work, work."

Lucas laughed, too. It was a nice sound.

We walked back to the VW and things didn't seem quite so awful. School was beginning and we still knew how to laugh.

I wondered if there were any decent boys in the junior class. If they'd like me. If there would be a girlfriend or two for me — a girl who wouldn't laugh when I told her about homesickness, a girl who cared about clothes, and would let me use her makeup, and read her magazines, and invite me home to watch her TV.

Seven days, I told myself. And then school.

Chapter VII

Our stop was the sixth of nineteen that the bus made, so there were plenty of empty seats when Lucas and I got on for the first time. Inquisitive faces stared at us. My insides knotted up and I had a moment of absolute panic. Where to sit? Cling to Lucas? Force myself on one of these kids? They were all ages, kindergarten to senior high. I tried to see if the older kids sat in the back, or if there was some sort of seating arrangement that people would expect me to know, but my eyes felt blurry and I couldn't tell what to do.

"Hey," said a freckled girl in the very back of the bus. ("Hey" had turned out to be Southern for "hello.") "Come sit with me. A bunch of rotten boys will be getting on at the next stop and I need a girl to fill up my seat."

I sat with her gratefully and we introduced ourselves. "I'm Connie," she said, "and I'm a junior, too. You don't know how glad I am to have another junior girl on the bus. All last year I rode with a sixth grader."

I was so glad to be talking with her! I felt like a puppy wagging my tail.

"Who is that handsome hunk?" she said.

I looked around, eager to see a handsome young man.

Connie giggled. "Silly. The guy who got on with you."

Lucas? Lucas was this handsome hunk? I stared at him.

Well, his complexion had cleared and tanned in the sun, and he had gotten pretty fit and muscular working at heavy jobs for five months. But if there was one thing I didn't want to talk about, it was Lucas, who meant nothing more to me right now than the other half of a farm chore. "Oh, he's the kid of the other family farming with us," I said.

"You're the city people who moved down the lane from the Shields, then," said Connie. "How I'd love to be from the city. The day I graduate from high school I'm headed for Atlanta. Or maybe Nashville. I want to work for an airline or a bank."

"There's quite a difference."

"I've got two years to make up my mind. So how do you like it here?"

I didn't want to risk offending anybody who was a native, even a native who yearned for a city. "The mountains are beautiful," I said, which was certainly true. "But I get homesick sometimes."

"Me, too. My parents divorced and when mother remarried we moved here. Two and a half years ago now. This is my stepfather's hometown. I like Valley High, but sometimes I'm so home-sick for Tennessee I could cry."

"I *do* cry," I said.

That was all it took: five minutes conversation between bus stops and Connie and I were friends.

It was an incredible relief to have a friend. In the next several weeks nothing meant more to me than sitting with Connie on the bus, during class, at lunch.

Connie could understand so much that I couldn't say to my parents. My parents just confused me with all their joy and exuberance. And I couldn't tell them what my feelings were without hurting theirs. As for Lucas, with whom Connie felt I should be discussing all this, since we shared it, well, he was certainly no longer an enemy (you can't be an active enemy of the person who's holding the chain saw when you're holding the log), but he wasn't exactly a friend either.

Connie showed me around, introduced me, got me started with lots of other girls, and all in all, being a newcomer in school turned out to be something of an asset. There were hardly any rough moments, and no lonely ones.

The homesickness didn't go away, though. It moved to the back of my body, sort of, coming out when I least expected it, like indigestion.

The boys in the junior class were polite and nice. Everybody said sir or ma'am to the teachers, and held doors for the girls, and complimented me on my pretty blouses. But nobody even hinted at wanting to ask me for a date. And since we had no telephone, nobody could have a sudden whim to call me to chat, or ask about homework, or invite me anywhere.

I wanted so much to be part of a group. Any group. Gathering after school for hamburgers, or rehearsing for a play, or practicing for a ballgame. But after class, I had to catch the bus and go home to do chores.

Sometimes when I thought about the dating ladder I'd be on if I were back home I'd have to choke back tears, and I'd feel dowdy and plain and boring. I had to train myself not to think of home when I was in school.

Lucas seemed to walk into the senior class and take over as Big Man On Campus. I wondered once if it surprised him as much as it surprised me.

But he never went anywhere, either. He had as many chores waiting at the farm as I did.

Connie was often sick with severe allergy problems, so at least one day a week I'd get on the bus and there'd be no Connie. I couldn't even phone to say I hoped she'd be better, because we had no phone. I'd sit on the bus with a little fourth grader named Eloise, who always wanted me to check her math homework.

In October, Susannah wrote to say she'd been to a dance at a nightclub and was going up to a fraternity party at Syracuse with a boy she'd met who was a really good-looking number and so suave, and she was trying for early acceptance to college.

I knew only nine people at Valley who wanted to go to college, and two of them were Lucas and me.

Lucas and I hopped off the bus one day to hike up the lane for home when he said, "Marnie, they've asked me to be on the basketball team."

Nobody had asked me to be on anything. "You aren't athletic," I said. "It's all you can do to walk on the bottoms of your feet."

"Very funny, Marnie."

"They didn't really ask you, Lucas. They had a class assignment in sarcasm."

"Of which I suppose you're the teacher," he said.

I knew I was being ugly and unfair to him. I knew I should congratulate him and tell him how much he'd changed for the better. But I couldn't. Just thinking of teams made me think of cheerleading back home and how that was closed to me forever. "Don't get excited about it," I said to Lucas. "They only want you because you're tall, and Valley men tend to be short."

"I can always count on you for an encouraging word, can't I?" He walked on ahead, his long legs covering the ground half again as fast as mine.

Lucas has changed for the better, I thought. I've gotten worse.

At dinner Lucas brought up the basketball team, but our parents merely looked confused and annoyed. "You can't be on a team," they said. "There's practice time, evening games, all sorts of precious time wasted by that sort of thing. We need you for the apples."

If it had been me I'd have had a tantrum.

Lucas merely accepted it without arguing. I guess he knew that they really did need him for the orchard and that the way we'd chosen to live — or they'd chosen — didn't leave space for basketball teams.

Instead, after school, we'd throw down our books, change into our oldest jeans and jackets, and head for the orchards. Endlessly we plucked apples, using little basketlike prongs on a long stick, filling bushels, loading the bushels on the tractor-drawn trailer, arguing about who got to stop picking apples for fifteen minutes and take the bushels back to the barn.

In school my favorite class was study hall. I never studied. I just sat there and let my eyes glaze over, sleeping awake, more or less.

We sold our apples to a man who had a huge refrigerated storage barn and we made enough to break even and cover the beginning costs of running the orchard for the next year, but we didn't make enough to live on over the winter.

So from the middle of November until spring, Mother, Aunt Ellen, and I baked bread, pies, and cakes for the mountain resort on the far side of the village. You have to bake an awful lot to earn anything resembling money. I wanted new school clothes so much, and my clothes from sophomore year were not only tight and short, but out of style — at Valley, girls wore much more conservative styles: a lot of pullover sweaters over oxford shirts. "I need new everything," I said, "most of all shoes."

Mother sewed a few things for me, but as for the rest, "You want them, you earn them," she told me flatly. So I made specialties of sweet potato pie, apple turnovers, and apple crisps. It took me till January to earn a shopping spree. Lucas drove me into the county seat, a town about twenty miles away, where they featured a sixteen-shop mall arranged around an indoor fountain. We both nearly died at the prices. "It was a lot more fun when I had a clothing allowance and went to Bloomingdale's," I said.

Lucas looked longingly at a pair of sneakers (thirty-four dollars) and I wanted the makeup kit in the tortoise shell case for thirty-six. We bought sneakers at the dime store for a dollar eighty-nine and I took lipstick from a brand x rack for fifty-nine cents. "I don't see what's so neat about being poor," I said. "Why do our parents want to live like this?"

"They had money, Marnie. It didn't make them happy. Working on the farm does. They love it, every minute of it. They really don't much care that they're broke." There was a sadness in Lucas' voice that stopped me short. I was peevish, I complained a lot, sometimes I was really miserable, but whatever Lucas' emotion was, it was much deeper than mine. It made me feel like a little girl, as if Lucas understood things I never would, and anger boiled up in me at all the things I was missing, and I stomped back to the car.

* * *

That winter we warmed our house with wood Lucas and I had cut and split. We popped popcorn that I grew, harvested, dried, and stored. The flowers on the table my mother had grown and dried hanging from the kitchen rafters. With her new loom, Aunt Ellen wove a beautiful tablecloth.

Our first Christmas on the farm we had roast duck (our own), sweet and white potatoes, beans, beets, stewed tomatoes (our canning), three kinds of bread, homemade cheese, and three kinds of pie. Everything from our own gardens and hands. Mother gave me a beautiful pantsuit she'd sewn during her spare time (I'd never noticed any spare time lying around!). It was a dark yellow denim, with a tiny bit of embroidery on the lapel. Lucas got the magazine subscriptions he'd been pining for. My parents bought each other things like butter presses and extra kerosene lanterns, and spent the whole day laughing delightedly.

The barn cat sneaked into the kitchen to have kittens under the sink and by evening the first snow was falling.

Even I had to admit there had never been such a beautiful Christmas.

"I'm going to build a solar greenhouse," said Lucas, brandishing a library book with blueprints and instructions. "Raise tomatoes so we can have fresh ones for salad in the dead of winter."

"Lucas, I canned at least forty million tomatoes. Have mercy. There's nothing I want less than more tomatoes. Raise flowers."

Aunt Ellen began teaching me to use the loom and I wove a slightly crooked placement.

Our goat had kids and we bought another couple of goats, too, because we'd found a health food store that would buy everything made of goats' milk that we could sell them.

"Marnie," said Connie. "If I tell you a secret, will you promise not to tell anybody?"

"Sure."

"Julie Fitzhugh has a crush on Lucas."

"On *Lucas*?"

"Oh, Marnie, just because you never notice him! He's the handsomest thing in this school. He's so tall and strong and he knows about absolutely anything you can think of. From French literature to how to build hen coops. From Phoenician civilization to fixing tractors. And he's always so courteous and calm and nice, and he has that marvelous smile."

I actually turned around in the school bus to have another look at Lucas.

"Does he date anyone, Marnie?" Connie wanted to know.

"No. He's never had time, I guess. Or the money." I thought of Susannah's dating ladder. I'd fallen off it, but Lucas never even had a chance to get on. He hadn't been dating back home and here he couldn't get started, although obviously he was very popular.

"Julie wanted to know if you've ever held hands with Lucas."

"Once. When we were both reaching for the same chicken egg."

"Ah. Romance," said Connie.

It was twenty-six degrees out and snowing and the wind was blowing off the mountains as if it wanted to strip our hill of its apple trees. And I had to walk outside to use the bathroom. Halfway between the house and my destination, I looked up into the falling snow and yelled at the whistling wind, "I hate this damn outhouse! Someday I'm going home! To a city, where people know how to live. Where you date. And walk on sidewalks. And the milk comes in cartons. And the bathrooms are inside!"

The snow kept falling and the outhouse was colder than ever.

One blustery January day when the school bus was late, and I'd stepped in an icy puddle and discovered a hole in my boots (the boots we couldn't afford to replace), and Lucas had lost a glove and had one hand balled up in his pocket, taking it out now and then to huff on it, he said suddenly, "Marnie, let's run away."

"Great idea. Where shall we go? Bahamas? Virgin Islands?"

"No airfare. Don't you have any loving relatives who'd give us shelter?"

"Two of them. They live down the lane in a drafty farmhouse with your two loving relatives."

"Oh. You mean those back-to-the-land types."

"Right. The ones whose hearts are pure and whose sweat is honest."

"And whose teenagers are rebellious."

We laughed. When the bus came, Connie wasn't there again, and I sat with Lucas for the very first time. For the very first time, we talked, not about goats or wood, but about ourselves. "I was sort of hoping the whole experiment would be doomed to failure," I said.

"Me, too. So far there are no signs of adult enthusiasm wearing thin."

"Well, hang in there, Lucas. Only six more months and you'll be off at college somewhere."

The pain I'd seen on his face before settled back in. His features turned bleak and miserable. "I'm not going to college, Marnie," he said simply. "They can't make a success of the orchard without another full-time worker. And the only one around for free is me."

"Not go to college? But your whole life had been a preparation for college!"

"Dad says college merely leads to a diploma that is but a piece of paper. Meaningless. Superficial. I'm an adult now, he says, and I'm needed at home with my family, helping to earn the daily bread."

"Oh, Lucas, how terrible! Did they make it an order? You have to stay?"

"No, they wouldn't do that. I'm eighteen now and I don't think they could force me to stay. Or that they want to use force. But they can't give me a dime and you can't go to college, even local state colleges, without an awful lot of dimes. Besides, they're right, they do need me."

"Oh, Lucas!" My heart ached for him. I could hardly stand to see the slump that had taken over not just his posture, but his face as well. I'd have hugged him, patted him, if it would have helped. But he didn't need me. He needed a different future.

Lucas shrugged, leafing through his school-books with a detached longing. For Lucas, learning was something exciting. College had meant knowledge all around him, spilling out of books and professors and laboratories and libraries, waiting for him to scoop it up. And now learning was going to stop here, with a high school reader.

"Are you going to stay, then?" I asked.

"I suppose so. I owe it to my parents, I guess."

I remembered Eve — so long ago it seemed like another world — saying Lucas' profile was fine, it was his personality that worried her. It seemed to me that both his profile and his personality were in pretty good shape. It would be an incredible sacrifice for him to stay, and from what I knew of the way he'd behaved all year, he'd do it cheerfully, too. Not bothering the adults with his complaints. Not like Marnie, who drowned people in complaints. "What did you want to study at college, Lucas?"

"Literature. Wanted to be a college professor."

A year ago I'd have said he looked like a college professor. Sort of weedy and bookwormy. But not now.

"But I'm not sure anymore," he said, surprising me. "Farming really has opened my eyes to a lot of things. I don't want to be a farmer, but sometimes I think I've learned as much working around those apple trees as I would have sitting around a library. In a way, there's a lot more satisfaction learning things by struggling with them, right there, in the field, than by reading about them." He laughed a little. "Although I don't relish thinking about being here on the farm permanently. I suppose if I really get desperate, I can always join the Army."

"I thought you were a pacifist."

"I've decided that nobody who can behead his own chickens and ducks is a pacifist." He sighed, fingers stroking his calculus text. "And now that I think of it," he said, obviously making himself be lighthearted again, "the Army may use outhouses, too."

"How uncivilized of them," I said. "I'm sure you're wrong. I think trenches were left behind in the First World War."

"Different kind of trench, ding-a-ling," said Lucas, standing up to get off the bus. He grinned at me, made a fist, and gave my nose a gentle tap. And by the time he'd turned away, the strangest thing had happened to me.

I'd fallen in love with Lucas Peterson.

Chapter VIII

It was embarrassing to be in love with Lucas.
Every time I remembered all the dreadful
things we had said about him back home, I'd get
flushed and hot. That first week this happened so
often my mother noticed and wanted to know if
I was coming down with something. "No," I said,
thinking that I had already come down with it.

It seemed ridiculous to me that I could be
head over heels in love with someone for whom
I'd had no use all my life. (Head over heels, it
turned out, was a good description — I felt fizzy,
as if I'd been carbonated!) And it happened so
quickly. No warning buzzers, no premonitions of
fate, no foreshadowings of things to come the way
they do in Gothics. Just a silly remark and a grin
and I was caught up in emotions I'd never had
before.

It was no wonder they called this a "crush." It
sat there in the front of my mind, and smushed
everything else. My thoughts of Lucas were so

constant and so heavy they weighted me down at the same time that I was fizzing.

It was, all in all, a wonderful feeling.

It would have been even more wonderful if Lucas had noticed.

He was oiling the hinges on the barn door. "Can I help?" I said. How handsome he was, bent over that hinge, oil dripping down onto his fingers.

"Oh, did you want to do this?" he said. "Great." He handed the oil can to me. "Do all the doors and the barnyard gates, too. Now I can get to that broken well pump handle."

And off he strode. Out of sight. Leaving me with oil dripping down *my* fingers, which was for some reason not a handsome thing at all, but infuriating.

He tore a hole in his favorite sweater and I said, "Here, I'll darn the hole," taking the sweater from him. Aunt Ellen said, "Lord have mercy, did I hear Marnie actually make an offer to mend something?" Everyone laughed except Lucas, who was already back in his bedroom getting another sweater. Aunt Ellen mended it after all, because when I tried I just made lumps.

I brushed my hair more. I changed my clothes more. Lucas said, "You're going to bring in wood wearing *that*?"

We'd said back home that Lucas had a voice like a newborn foghorn. But Lucas' frame had expanded to fit the voice, and now it was a fine deep baritone like a TV commentator's. I daydreamed about how "I love you" would sound in Lucas' beautiful voice. I didn't even hear "I like you." He spoke to the goats more than he talked to me.

Mother announced that she wanted to have roast chicken for dinner, which meant killing and plucking the chicken. That's something you don't fully realize when you first raise animals: that they're going to be quite hard to eat if nobody kills them. For a while you decide to be a vegetarian. For a while you go right on raising the chickens but you drive downtown and buy your chicken meat at the grocery, where it's all neatly wrapped and somebody else killed it. After that you get your neighbor Mr. Shields to do it for you in exchange for eggs. Eventually you get somewhat hardened to it and you learn to do it yourself. The six of us always tried to be gone when it was chicken-slaughter time. In fact, Aunt Ellen got migraines quite regularly whenever meat was on the menu and my father invariably found he'd made an urgent appointment with . . . with . . . well, he couldn't remember, but it was urgent.

"I'll do it," sighed Lucas.

I wanted so much to be with Lucas I actually volunteered to do it with him. "Job's all yours," said Lucas. "Give my regrets to the hens."

"I wanted to do it with you, not for you," I said, but he was long gone.

I did get to help Lucas build his solar greenhouse. This consisted of Lucas muttering and stewing over his blueprints and his lists, making careful marks on his lumber and saying to me, "Hold it higher, Marnie." "No, Marnie, no, for pete's sake, *this* end."

This association came to a bloody end because I was so busy daydreaming about Lucas' beautiful strong hands and how they would feel holding mine that I nailed his palm instead of the butt joint. After a trip to the hospital and a tetanus shot and some stitches, Lucas was not terribly thrilled to have my help anymore.

One afternoon Lucas didn't get on the school-bus.

He's run away, I thought. He couldn't take it anymore, and he left.

Without me, I thought. He asked me to run away with him. I should have taken him up on it.

But he wouldn't actually have wanted me along. Lucas and I were barely friends, let alone ready to run off together. He never confided in me, with the single exception of that conversation on the bus, when he'd been so down he'd even been willing to talk to me.

I remembered every single mean crack I'd ever made to Lucas, and there were quite a lot of them. If only I could have a recall, the way they do cars from Detroit.

I wondered just what Lucas really did think of me. As the girl who put holes in his hand? The girl who shoveled out the chicken coop? The girl who got in his way and took up his space and insulted him?

I poked around the house all afternoon, worrying about where he'd gone, wondering if I'd ever see him again. I didn't dare say anything to our parents. They might call the police, or the principal, or almost anything. I'd long given up predicting their moves.

I found myself in my little loft, wrapped in the quilt that was my only reliable friend, crying because I'd finally found the nicest boy anywhere, and he not only wasn't interested in me — he was gone.

Lucas walked in about seven o'clock, with two young goslings in his arms. He'd gotten them free from a farmer miles away and had hitchhiked back to our farm. Hitchhiking isn't easy at any time and apparently even fewer drivers are eager to pick up a kid in old jeans carrying baby geese. That, explained Lucas to those of us who were interested, was what took so long.

Because baby anythings have to be kept very warm (we'd learned that the hard way), Lucas got a big cardboard box which he filled with wood shavings and all our hot water bottles. "Electric light bulb would be better," he said meaningfully to our parents. But they didn't rush out to get the house wired. "This way," said Lucas, "I'll have to get up at least twice during the night and refill these bottles." I thought of interrupting our much-needed sleep to heat water on the woodstove and refill hot water bottles for two little geese.

"These," said Lucas, looking each of us very carefully in the eye, "are going to be my pets. They are not for Easter dinner, right?"

"Right," we chorused. I wanted to volunteer myself as a pet for Lucas, but from the way he looked at his goslings he had better things available.

Every night Lucas got up and refilled his hot water bottles and clucked to his goslings. It was quite depressing. You can hover over me, I thought. But he didn't. "I'll heat the water for you tonight," I said. "You get some sleep."

"Oh, would you?" he said eagerly. "That's terrific, Marnie, thanks."

I actually loved getting up twice that night to keep his old goslings toasty. I did it for three weeks, until Lucas decided the geese were tough enough to last without the extra heat. Every morning Lucas would say "thank you" and my heart would fall out of my rib cage during his smile, and every morning my father would say, "What are you doing, Lucas? Blackmailing the girl? You couldn't get me up twice a night for a pair of geese we don't even get to eat." I would blush, Lucas would shrug, laughing, and we'd go off to school.

Unfortunately, Lucas' legs were much longer than mine and we didn't walk to the bus stop together. It seemed to me that when a girl kept your geese warm, you should at least walk her to the bus stop.

Lucas needs a book of etiquette, I thought. I shall write him one. *When warming geese . . .*

Lucas' birthday came in March.
I taught myself how to knit, using a book

85

Connie's mother loaned me, and made a sweater for Lucas. I used a natural-colored wool from Scotland that took so much money from my baking income the sweater had to be perfect. I'd knit on the bus, during study hall, and in my loft.

It was a pullover with a thick turtleneck. Most of it was plain stockinette stitch, but there were three cable columns. I was scared of the cables at first, but Connie's mother was right: Cables are fun and you feel so competent when they actually cross over and loop.

I had it done two days before his birthday.

"What a shame you got the gauge wrong and it won't fit you after all," said my mother, hugging me to comfort me. "You're so nice to give it to Lucas, after all that work. Or you could give it to your father. His birthday is next month, he's the same size, and he needs one, too."

"Oh, I might as well give it to Lucas," I said. "Get it out of the way."

My father gave Lucas a Swiss Army knife with lots of little blades and things. Mother had made him a leather vest. Aunt Ellen got him thick, strong workboots. Uncle Bob had bought about twenty books at a church yard sale and also a new flashlight with lots of batteries. And then Lucas took up the last package. It didn't say it was from me. It was just a fat, soft present wrapped in plain brown paper with a sagging yarn bow. He opened it eagerly. "Mother, it's beautiful!" he exclaimed. "I love it."

"I didn't make it," said Aunt Ellen.

"You didn't make it?" he repeated. He looked totally bewildered.

"Marnie made it."

"*Marnie made it?*" He stared at me as if he'd never seen me before. I tried to look appealing. Lucas looked back at the sweater, stuck a finger through a cable loop, and stared at me again. "I — I didn't know you could knit," he said at last.

I nodded mutely.

"Well, try it on, Lucas," said his mother.

Lucas put it on. I held my breath. It fit beautiful. He couldn't, I said to myself, have bought a nicer sweater anywhere. You can't even see where I got the cables reversed and Connie's mother ripped out fifty-two rows and got me started up again the right way. "Gee, thanks, Marnie," said Lucas. He had a rather worried look on his face. Maybe the sweater was itchy.

"You're welcome," I said.

"Must have been a lot of work."

"Yes. It was."

There was an awkward silence. And then Uncle Bob, whom I had hitherto considered merely a driver of tractors or a cutter of trees, said, "Hey. She keeps your geese for you. She knits sweaters for you. Is something afoot I don't know about?"

Everybody, including Lucas, even including me, laughed. "Nonsense," said my mother. "The sweater started out to be for Marnie herself, but it turned out too large, so she ended up giving it to Lucas."

"Oh," said everybody. "Isn't that just like farming? Always turns out harder or different than you thought."

I thought of all those hours of knitting — and nothing was different. Lucas didn't know it was a labor of love, he thought it was a mistake.

I wanted to pull him aside and tell him, hug him, kiss him, do anything that would show him how I felt.

But I was afraid to. He'd be polite about it. What could be worse than spilling out your heartbreak and having all that emotion met with courtesy?

Lucas tugged his jacket over my sweater, grinned at all of us equally, and went out to check on the animals.

Chapter IX

I tried to stop myself from being in love with Lucas.

It was obviously a lost cause and they say you shouldn't bat your head on brick walls for fear of permanent damage to said skull.

So I dedicated time to remembering Joel, but he hadn't written since last July, and I'd spent a lot more time with Lucas than I ever had with Joel. My picture of Joel would blur like a movie changing scenes and Lucas would be superimposed on it. I'd find myself smiling dreamily to myself until somebody would say, "Marnie, stop your giggling and get on with your work."

Susannah wrote a very long letter I read constantly to keep my mind on things other than Lucas. She had gone to a terrific party where they danced to a live band, and she dated the drummer who was really cute, who introduced her to a college fraternity man who invited her to Yale for a weekend, and life was perfect and how was I?

I, I'd think, am in love with Lucas Peterson. How's that for laughs, Susannah? Lucas doesn't even know I'm alive. If he thinks of me at all, it's because he needs a human sawhorse for his lumber cutting or he wants a hunk of homemade bread.

Susannah, pity me.

Lucas probably thinks I'm his *sister*.

Susannah, we pump buckets of water together and I'm thinking how strong and lithe he is and he's looking off at the horizon dreaming of college, probably, and other girls. We feed the goats together and I'm thinking how nice and funny he is and he's rubbing the *goat* under the chin. Not once has he ever stopped to think that maybe I wouldn't mind having *my* chin rubbed. Or kissed. We clean the kerosene lamps together and I'm thinking how handsome he is and he's repeating math formulas to himself because he has a test the next day.

I'm thinking of knitting another sweater for him, Susannah. I'll include a letter saying, *I am not your sister. Take another good, long look. Love, Marnie.* I'll draw arrows toward the word love. Include some candy kisses.

Or maybe I'll just give the sweater to my father. Lucas would think it was pretty weird that a crabby old girl he happened to live with would knit him two sweaters.

Connie had a Welcome Spring Slumber Party.

It was the first time in precisely one year that

I'd spent a night in a house with a real bathroom. Two real bathrooms, in fact: one brown and beige tiled, and the other pale blue and white tiled. Featuring paired taps, one of which said, HOT. Connie's mother was really quite understanding when I said I'd rather take a hot, soaking bath in the blue tub than pull taffy with the other girls.

I watched television for the first time in months, but I couldn't even follow the plot of this show that everybody had been talking about and I had never seen, because daydreaming about dumb old Lucas was so much more absorbing. "Marnie," said Connie, "what is your problem?"

I knew she would understand (she was deep in the throes of a crush on her cousin's college roommate), but somehow it was too private to share.

Evenings when Lucas and I sat together at the cleared and cleaned kitchen table to do our homework, I'd try to think of a way to get Lucas to talk to me.

It was so ironic. Lucas had always been the one boy I'd had no trouble talking to. An endless stream of wisecracks had come out of me. But back then, I hadn't cared about Lucas. It was quite unfair that I could babble with someone who didn't count, and be tonguetied with him when he did count.

"How's your homework, Lucas?"

"Well, you know. Homework." He'd go on scribbling.

"Isn't it nice that spring seems finally to be coming?"

91

"Marnie, I really have to study. D'you mind?"

It was getting to be boring being in love with Lucas. I'd ache and he'd ignore.

One night Lucas was bent over his calculus worksheets, muttering to himself, writing, erasing, sighing, and running his fingers through his hair. He kept making faces at the answers he got. His fingers were thicker and longer than mine, his arms and hands covered with fine blond hair that looked like frosting against his deep tan. Even in winter he had kept his tan, because he still worked outdoors so much, and the work was so demanding that even in chilly weather he'd often strip off his shirt. Winter in North Carolina, unlike winter back home, often had breaks: sunny warm days like spring, piercing the doldrums of February and March with welcome frequency.

There was no doubt in my mind that Michelangelo would have been honored to sculpt Lucas without his shirt. I thought it very nice of winter to have warm spells.

I ceased to do my own homework and admired Lucas across the table. He'd started shaving. The faint, raspy patches on his cheeks would be different from any texture I'd ever felt. I was sitting there half gasping, sighing to myself, when Lucas looked up and said, "You getting a cold, Marnie?"

"No." My teeth began to chatter.

"It's pretty warm in here," said Lucas, looking at me doubtfully. "I mean, April outside and the stove in here still hot from supper."

I gave him what was meant to be a reassuring smile which came out an absolutely stupid, empty-headed grin wrapped around teeth that kept right on chattering.

Lucas looked at me the way he might look at a dripping faucet he couldn't shut off. If we had faucets, that is. "If you're cold," he said finally, "wear my sweater." It was the one I'd knit for him. He'd just taken it off and draped it over the back of his chair. Lucas handed it to me across the table and I pulled it on over my head. While my face was hidden underneath the sweater, I sniffed the wool. Sure enough, it smelled faintly of Lucas.

I pulled the sweater down all the way and kind of snuggled inside it. The next thing I knew I was laughing, doubled over laughing. I had really hit rock bottom when I had to get my fun sniffing old wool!

How simple it would be if I could just say, "Lucas, old man, I'm crazy about you."

Immediately I was afraid I would actually say that, and Lucas would cringe, or run away, or call a parent to rescue him. I chewed the insides of my lips to keep myself from telling Lucas I loved him and all the time I was still giggling away.

Lucas regarded me irritably. Finally, he said that he thought he would just do his homework in the living room and I could giggle peacefully to myself here alone in the kitchen, okay?

And then it wasn't funny anymore. It was awful. I really did love Lucas. But I was nothing but a nuisance to him. A younger sister sort of pain who was in the way except when she was caring for his geese.

I sat at my table and the history book blurred in front of me. Be calm, I told myself. Be adult and rational about this. Your whole crush is silly and pointless. You can handle your feelings better than this.

Spring came in jerks. A week of mild, balmy weather and a week of icy rain. Two days of sun and heat and an evening of wet snow that didn't stick. Like my heart. Every time I looked at Lucas, it jerked.

I had classes, homework, baking, weaving, kindling to gather, water to carry, laundry to hang out, chickens to feed.

With all that work it should have been easy to put Lucas out of my mind.

It wasn't.

I began looking very carefully at my mother. We had not talked — really talked — since I could remember. For years I was too small, and then, abruptly, too busy. Empty whirlwind, they'd accused me when we left the city.

They were right, I thought.

But I was afraid to start talking to Mother. What if I told her about Lucas and she laughed? What if she called to everybody else to come and hear the funniest thing in eighty-five years? What if she said, "I told you so, Marnie"? What if she said something useless like, "These things work out, dear"?

Besides, I didn't really want to talk. I wanted to look at Lucas and find him looking right back at me and know from the stars in his eyes that he wasn't just searching for someone to take over the hoeing.

"The geese," said Lucas, "like you better than they like me."

It was true. When we got home from school, the geese would honk and flap their wings and come skittering over the barnyard to stand by the fence corner to greet us. Lucas got there first, because he walked so fast, but they'd pay only token attention to him. They'd wait for me to get there. Then they'd honk some more and stick their beaks through the wire, and I'd pat them, and talk baby talk, and usually go through the gate and let them walk around me, and we'd have a sort of geesy conversation. "I'm sorry," I said. "I didn't do it on purpose."

Lucas laughed. "I'm not complaining. I'm just commenting."

"You're not changing your mind, are you?" I said anxiously.

"About what?"

"About these geese."

"What about the geese, Marnie?" He was obviously forcing himself to be patient.

"You're not going to want to eat them, are you?"

"Of course not. I'm crazy about these geese. The books said geese would be fun and they are. I was just mentioning that they like you best, which they do."

And he went on into the house.

We had a lot of conversations like that. Friendly. Even nice. But not romantic. And Lucas didn't keep them up for very long. And they certainly didn't lead to a date.

But then, why would Lucas want to date me? If he started feeling romantic toward a girl, he'd want someone he didn't associate with farm chores. Someone, I thought gloomily, like that Julie. Her father's a banker. The only animal she's ever had is a manicured toy poodle. The only kind of water she uses comes out of a tap. The only bread she eats comes from the grocery shelf.

Sounds great! I thought. When do we start?

"Marnie, come into the kitchen! The resort sent a message that they're catering a special pre-wedding party and they need six hundred sweet rolls. We've got work to do!"

I saved a sweet roll for Lucas and took it to him with a cup of hot tea, which we'd all learned to like once coffee went beyond our budget. He was fastening the glass panels on his greenhouse. "I'll have it ready just in time for summer heat," he said. "Oh, well. This fall I'll be glad to have it."

I handed him the treat.

"Thanks, Marnie," he said, not even looking up. "Set it down, I'll have it later."

It's called being dismissed.

I trudged wearily back to the kitchen to knead another huge mound of dough.

There was a senior prom, of course. I guess every high school has a senior dance. "Are you going, Lucas?" I said.

"And wear what? My barn boots? My blue jeans with the hole in the knee? My flannel shirt with the patches on the elbows?"

It was the very first time I'd heard any bitterness in Lucas' voice. None of our parents picked up on it, which made me feel slightly closer to Lucas. At least I understood, even if he wouldn't let me share.

"Lucas doesn't like dancing," said Aunt Ellen. "Every Friday when he was ten and eleven I forced him to go to ballroom dancing lessons. One Friday he ground to a halt outside the dance floor and said, 'Mother, if I have to go in here once more, I will walk out the other side and you will never see me again,' and he sounded so certain that I said, 'Then we'd better go home,' and as far as I know Lucas has never danced since."

"Have you?" I asked him.

"Nope. Always seemed like a stupid exercise."

"That's what you thought about basketball and now you love gym."

"True. I suppose there's a remote possibility I

might come to love dancing if it were forced on me three times a week. However, I doubt if the problem will come up." He bent over to tie up his high boots, pulling the laces tight, aware of his ankles instead of mine. He went on out to the barn, and that was that for my chance at a senior prom with Lucas Peterson.

Chapter X

"Marnie?" said my mother.

I grinned at her. We were making soap. There is nothing less fun to me than making soap. It's a terrible, smelly, dangerous job, and all I can ever think of is how red my hands are getting and how for fifty-nine cents I could just buy two bars of the stuff.

But we were outdoors, and it was the end of April, and the apple trees on the hill were pink and white with bloom against an emerald green meadow, and a few dozen yards away from me, Lucas was painting the board fence.

From their side of the wire-lined boards, the goats, geese, chickens, cow — yes, we got a cow — watched with great interest. From my side, I watched with greater interest. I loved seeing Lucas bend, reach, and stretch, dipping the brush, or wiping his hands on a rag I'd found for him. My rag, I'd think, going maudlin over an old torn blouse with paint daubs on it.

"Yes, Mother?"

"You're different." She said it firmly, nodding to herself as if this were a prize at the fair. "A lot of the things we hoped for when we came here have happened to you. You're more thoughtful. Slower. Easier to live with. Do you — do you feel different?"

"Yes, I guess I do."

"Is it a better feeling, or a worse one?"

"I don't know, Mother. I really don't." I wanted to add that having a crush on Lucas was certainly complicating the issue.

"Do you like the farm at least a little now?" she said wistfully.

It was so difficult to know how to answer when she or my father asked me things like that. I couldn't bring myself to hurt their feelings with my real feelings. Anyway, I hardly ever knew what my real feelings were.

The farm was not home for me. Home still meant a warm yellow apartment on the eleventh floor, with a view of a sprawling city, and all that the word "city" implies.

Yet nothing tugged at my heart more than the sight of our orchard in bloom, or my own newborn ducklings taking their first walk. Nothing except Lucas, that is.

I felt as if the farm had taught me a thousand lessons that my parents had been right in guessing I needed to learn.

But I *had* learned them.

I'd gotten straight A's, in fact, and now I deserved to graduate. To go back to the city (by now, I'd have settled for any city) where I belonged.

Yet Lucas was here, accepting his responsibilities, for at least another year, and I was settled at Valley High. And when the scenery included Lucas peeling off his shirt again because the sun was so hot, I had to admit that there was no place I'd rather be than right here, making soap, watching him.

For a moment I considered pulling off *my* shirt. That should attract a little attention of the non-sisterly variety.

"Yes," I said to my mother, laughing at myself, "I guess I like it here."

She hugged herself with delight. (She couldn't hug me because I was pouring the lye.)

We talked about the farm, or rather, she talked and I listened. Lyrically she told me of all the things that made her so happy. Me, for instance. Seeing me smile so much. The chores like soapmaking. Cheesemaking. Seeing the trees in bloom. Having the companionship that only very hard work and good results can bring between people. "Is it spring?" said my mother. "Or the farm? Or school? Or what?"

"What do you mean?" I said

"Making you smile so often. Every time I glance your way, you seem to have this private little pleasure about something."

I added a few small sticks to the fire under the soap kettle.

I checked the lye.

I stared at my feet.

Finally I said, "Well, I have this crush on this boy."

"Marnie, how nice! April and young love. It's perfect. Who is he?"

I couldn't go into details. She would know there weren't too many intellectual, yet agriculturally knowledgeable, six-foot, eighteen-year-old blonds around. "He's super," I said.

She giggled. "I remember when I fell in love for the first time. It was with my best friend's date and I was never able to tell a single soul. I pined for that boy for months."

"Did you like being in love?"

"I'm in love right now, Marnie. With your father and this farm."

That was how she was going to be. I went back to the soap.

"But you mean the first parts of love, don't you? I guess the answer would be yes and no. Being in love is awfully time-consuming."

"I've noticed."

"Sometimes it seems as if life doesn't contain anything but that boy, and sometimes you feel as if anybody but you would handle the situation more intelligently. But it's a dizzy, swooping sort of thing, to be in love. Like a barn swallow, I've always thought."

We talked about love and crushes and kisses. She looked so young and happy, and so sort of romantic, in the kind of clothing she had started wearing once we moved to the farm, that it was like watching someone on TV, not at all like glancing over at my mother. We talked about her, though, not about me. I could tell Mother was dying to know more about my feelings, but didn't want to press me. Finally I said, "He doesn't know I'm alive."

Her face fell. "Marnie, how awful. I remember the plight well. How are you going to show him that you are alive?"

It was such a relief to see that she really understood and cared! I have an ally, I thought. "I don't know," I said. "It's definitely a problem."

"What matters to him? Clothing? Ballgames? Cars?"

"No, I don't think any of that appeals to him much."

"I like him already," said Mother, and we giggled the way Susannah and I used to giggle. Mother was biting her lips with pleasure.

"You're really enjoying this," I teased her.

"I love remembering the nice parts of growing up," she said. "There are a lot of small happy things, like having a crush."

"There's nothing small about it. And lots of times it isn't very happy, either."

We went back to the soap.

Lucas finished the portion of fence he was doing and moved over to the animals' side to paint. The goats nuzzled him with great interest, wanting to drink out of the paint can and lick his brush. One of the kids chewed happily on Lucas' trouser leg and the chickens skittered between his feet to see what everybody was so interested in. Lucas muttered and jerked and swung his legs gently at all of them to scatter them and they moved over an inch or so and started right in again on his legs.

I felt a certain envy. How come goats could nuzzle Lucas and I couldn't even talk to him?

"I'm trying to think how to solve your problem," said my mother. "This is the age of feminism, so maybe you could ask him for a date."

I could see myself leaning over the wet fence, shoving the nanny goat out of range, and asking Lucas if he wanted to go to the movies with me. I, who had no ticket money, no gas money, no driver's license, no time, and probably wasn't the girl he'd want to go with anyway.

"I could give you a little money," said my mother. "I always keep a bit hoarded away."

The use of money to achieve happiness is absolutely forbidden in our two families these days. I was really touched that she would think my crush important enough to be willing to break the rules and spend the precious money for it. How strange, I thought. Back in the city none of us would have thought twice about ten dollars here or twenty dollars there. Now it's a gift. A sacrifice.

"I do care, Marnie," said my mother softly. "And I remember how it feels."

"I can't drive," I said, shrugging off the idea. Actually I was afraid to ask Lucas. If he went with me — and he probably would — it would just be to get off the farm. It wouldn't be for the pleasure of my company.

"I know!" said Mother excitedly. "Lucas could

104

invite a date, too, and the four of you could double, and he would do the driving."

I blushed.

I couldn't stop myself from looking at Lucas, and blushing harder, looking away and then blushing again.

"Oh," said my mother. "Oh." She bit her lip again and began laughing very softly.

"It isn't funny!" I whispered furiously.

"Oh, no, honey, I agree, it isn't funny at all. I'm not laughing, if you know what I mean, I'm just kind of, well, I'm — "

"Laughing," I said sulkily.

"Because I love you. Because I love Lucas."

We made soap. It was my turn to stir. You have to stir at a distance to keep the lye fumes from reaching your nose and after a while your wrists ache and you risk getting careless.

We tested the mix for thickness. We still have trouble guessing when it's cooked enough. Our last soap batch separated. "I think it's right," said my mother dubiously. We added the coloring — Aunt Ellen had made a pink extract from boiled tulip blossoms — and the thick, dark tan soap turned a vague ruddy color. "Oh, well," said Mother. "Get ready."

We took our triple-folded potholders, turned the huge pot very carefully, and began to fill the rack of molds. We're both nervous that we're going to burn ourselves and we pour without breathing, so every time we tilt the pot back we gasp a little. When it was done we set the pot on gravel and stepped back, as relieved as if we'd just lived through major surgery.

"I think you're right, dear," said my mother.

"That we should just buy it?"

"Nonsense. That you're just part of the general endurance test here at the farm for Lucas. We do have a problem with Lucas, Marnie. How are we going to make him see a girl instead of the other half of a chore?"

"Oh, Mother, I try to help him with something and he says, 'No, thanks, Marnie, I can do it myself.' I try to help with something else and he says, 'Oh, did you want to do that? Great, then you do it and I'll go somewhere else and do something else.' "

Mother frowned. "How about school?"

"We don't have any classes together. Or even lunch. We sat together on the bus exactly once. He always sits with the boys and I always sit with Connie."

"Hmmmm. It doesn't sound too promising, does it? How do you feel about the direct approach? A little heart-to-heart talk with Lucas so he'll know how you feel?"

"Ugh."

"Why not?"

"Mother, I don't want to instruct him! I don't want to outline a romance for him. I want *him* to want it."

"True. Well, then, I guess the first thing is to get you two off together where you don't have a chore to share or animals or apples to worry about. Or school to interfere." She frowned even

106

more deeply, but it wasn't an angry frown. It was an I'm-giving-this-a-lot-of-thought frown. "He really is cute, isn't he?" she said, looking at the paint brush going back and forth over the white boards.

I agreed.

"I know, Marnie! We need some supplies from that store in Boone, the one that specializes in odd homesteading gear. Now, Boone is two hours away, which is four hours stuck in seats next to each other. Furthermore, there's lots to do in Boone. Restaurants. Movies. Hanging Rock Park. That little mountain railroad amusement park. I'll make up your shopping list, but you two can spend the whole day and evening there. You'd be having fun together, not just working side by side. And maybe you could take his hand and maybe he would realize you didn't *need* his hand, you just liked his hand."

"Yeah. The hand I put a nail through."

Mother exploded with giggles. "It'll be something to tell your grandchildren about, Marnie. See that dent in Grampa's hand?"

"Mother, I haven't even dated him and you have grandchildren here."

"I like to plan ahead."

We both giggled, like junior high girls in the back row when the teacher isn't looking. Lucas glanced up for a moment, saw nothing particularly amusing, and went back to his painting.

"You may not think farm life is ideal," said my mother, "but just look what it did for Lucas."

"I look, Mother," I said. "Believe me, I look."

Chapter XI

Lucas braked hard and took in his breath sharply. "Marnie," he said suddenly, reaching across the open space between our seats in the VW bus, and grabbing my hand. "Marnie, *what is that?*"

For a second I was actually scared. I looked around fearfully and then I burst out laughing. "Don't be afraid, son," I said robustly. "It's called a stoplight. I know you've never seen anything like it before, but it isn't vicious." I kept hanging onto his hand. What do you know, Mother was right that handholding would be step one!

"I wasn't sure," said Lucas. "The way it was blinking at me, way up on that wire, I thought it might leap, or attack us, or something."

Several cars behind us honked. "The natives are restless," I said.

"Perhaps I should move on, then."

The light *had* been green for some time.

"I usually require two hands to drive and change gears, Marnie."

I blushed, dropping his right hand. Lucas found a space in a parking lot behind a row of stores. We hopped out, locked up the bus, and stood marveling at the handsome asphalt. "Look at the way those white lines so neatly divide the place up into little car cubicles," said Lucas.

"Ah, civilization." I stooped to pick up somebody's litter. "I love you."

"Look at that," said Lucas. "Feast your eyes, Marnie. A neon sign."

"Urban blight," I observed. "City decay. Revolting."

"And I love it," said Lucas. "It's actually noisy here. Horns honking instead of geese."

"And that," I said, "that over there is something I've yearned for for thirteen months." I took his hand again and pulled him my way.

"What? I don't see anything."

"A traffic jam."

Lucas grinned. "Beats strawberry jam any day."

We stood on that corner, holding hands and laughing like fools for at least fifteen minutes. I am sure any passerby must have thought we were high on some vile, mind-bending drug. It would have been quite difficult to explain that a mere trip into a little country city (stretching my previous definition of city) had given us both a good fit of giggles.

"Do you see that criminal over there?" said Lucas, whispering and nudging me.

"No, where?"

"That woman with the three innocent little children."

"What's she doing to them?"

"She's buying them soda pop. And potato chips laced with preservatives! And sin of sins, Twinkies."

"Lucas, I have a confession to make."

"Confess, confess."

"I am being overcome by a deep, overwhelming need for a Twinkie."

"I just happen to have some money with me. May I offer the lady a Twinkie?"

We marched into the store and stood gazing at the racks of junk food. "I feel a twinge of guilt coming on," said Lucas. "My mother saying, we gave you our hard-earned money so you could betray our standards like this?"

"Is it just a twinge?" I said. "With determination, you can overcome a mere twinge."

So he bought two packs of Twinkies and we strolled down the main drag of Boone, happily chewing.

"Marnie, I have made a discovery," said Lucas.

"Please be so good as to reveal it."

Lucas stood over a trash basket, chained to the sidewalk — I could imagine our parents' reactions to a society where even the trash baskets would be stolen — and dropped in his second Twinkie. "Your sweet rolls are a lot better," he said. "Spoiled me."

I couldn't even say thank you. Getting a compliment from Lucas wrapped Scotch tape around my tongue, like old times. Don't let me freeze up, God. Please, I prayed, let me still be able to talk to him.

I spotted a sign with an arrow pointing to the college campus. I hadn't known Boone was a college town. I wondered if Lucas did; if thinking about college might ruin our day for us.

We went into a handcrafts shop to check out their wares, but there wasn't much there we didn't already have or couldn't make ourselves.

Next door was a ski apparel store, having a half-price, end-of-season sale. Even at that there was nothing we could afford. And, as Lucas pointed out, shiny, emerald-green ski vests didn't seem right for mucking out the stable.

We found a bookstore where Lucas wandered longingly up and down the aisles. I was amazed when he chose a book on carpentry instead of some of the new fiction. "I'm just not that interested in fiction right now," he explained. "I have so much more to learn about all the skills we need to make a success of that old orchard."

"Carpentry to make a success of the orchard? You going to build your own trees?"

"Well, no. Actually I want to make a special bed for myself, with built-in drawers and shelves and ledges. You don't know how I envy you having that nifty loft. I have that dark little closet at the back of the house and I have to share it with Mason jars. As soon as I figure out how to build my bed, I'm going to enclose the side porch and build in storage there so I can get that kitchen junk out of my room."

"You ought to paint your room. It's that dreary tan right now."

111

"I'm not good with colors. What do you think I should use?"

"It's so dark in there. I'd take a bright white enamel and one glossy trim color. Maybe a slick navy blue."

"Sounds good. I'll do that."

We had reached the store where our supplies could be purchased. It was a sort of general farm store, featuring everything from fireboxes to horse collars — old-fashioned things that mechanically equipped farmers don't have much need for. Much to our surprise, we found ourselves wandering around in there with more eagerness than we'd felt in any of the other stores. We were greatly taken with the tools that made jobs easier or quicker. "Look at this," I exclaimed. "A strawberry huller. A bean slicer. A corn kernel cutter. A cherry stoner."

"We don't have a cherry tree."

"Don't say it so loud. Your father will hear you and immediately plant a dozen."

Lucas and I found lamp wicks, a set of funnels, poultry shears, a chimney-cleaning brush, and a boot jack, crossing them off the list. We added grafting wax, a soil test kit, a manure fork which would be much easier to handle than the heavy old pitchfork we'd been using, and a new axe handle. I bought three pounds of coffee as my special splurge and Lucas chose a maximum-minimum thermometer.

"Would you believe I can't wait to get home and use this stuff?" said Lucas.

"I believe it. I've actually been hefting this manure fork and thinking what relief it'll be to use it."

"You've come a long way, baby," said Lucas.

We paid, took our purchases back to the VW, carefully locked the doors, and began wandering again. I bought a newspaper to see what was happening in town. "We could see a movie," said Lucas. "I used to love movies."

But there wasn't a decent movie playing.

"Then I vote for an indecent movie," said Lucas.

But none of them had matinees.

"Then let's check out the college," said Lucas. "I'm sure those are the dormitories, those brick buildings up on the hill."

It was a beautiful site, and the wind covered us with fresh, cold, clean air that was exhilarating to feel and to breathe in. When the path got very steep, I didn't have to reach for his hand, he took mine. He even slowed his normal walk so I didn't have to trot.

I was having a totally good time.

Classes were in session at the college. We walked down halls, hearing scraps of lectures. The place smelled of books and teachers and tests and unwilling test takers. By instinct Lucas found the library and we went in.

But it turned out that this library had closed stacks: if you didn't have student identification, you couldn't get at the books.

I guess for Lucas it was symbolic. He could

have a good time, but only up to a point. And then the door his parents and mine had constructed slammed on him.

No college for Lucas. No future for Lucas. None of the things he'd dreamed of, none of the goals he'd prepared for.

When we left the library the good mood was gone. Lucas walked fiercely, feet stomping, face set. He strode down the steep hill, away from the campus, back into town. I couldn't go as fast without running and I didn't want to run after him, like a little girl tagging along.

I wanted to say that I understood. That I knew how much our parents were demanding of him. Knew what he was giving up.

But if he had wanted a speech from me he wouldn't have stormed on ahead. I could call, yell for him to wait, and he would, he was too polite not to. If I said that walking faster than me was rude, he'd apologize, and he really would be sorry that he hadn't thought to slow down.

But then I'd know the only reason we were walking together was for courtesy's sake.

I did fine in school, but I was not, like Lucas, someone who loved school for school's sake. I too wanted college, but I was just as attracted by the boys and girls who'd be there with me (not to mention the running hot water in the dorms) as by the prospect of learning.

In my heart, I knew I'd be perfectly happy with an interesting job in a big bustling office in a city. I didn't need college the way Lucas did.

I stopped walking and just watched. He hadn't even noticed that I wasn't there. Too wrapped in his own thoughts. I didn't blame him — they were heavy thoughts, and no doubt he needed to be alone with them.

But it hurt.

Half in the sun and half under the weeping branches of a huge, gnarled, old cheery tree was a stone bench. I sat on it, feeling unspeakably tired and depressed. From blurry eyes I saw Lucas hike out of sight. I sat, mopping my tears with a handkerchief (we didn't use nice, convenient disposable paper tissues, not old-back-to-the-land us) and thinking how useless it was to have this crush on Lucas. Maybe I should tell him Julie liked him. Maybe that would be doing them both a favor.

That's when you know you're pretty far down. When you actually consider enlisting another girlfriend for the boy you love.

I don't know how long I sat there, head swirling with contradictory thoughts and hopes. An hour at least. Finally I stood up and headed for the lot where the VW bus was parked. Lucas was sitting motionless in the driver's seat, patiently waiting for me.

With no sarcasm, he said, "Have a good time?" I supposed he thought I'd been shopping or sightseeing.

"No." I climbed into the passenger side.

He hadn't expected that answer. He looked at me, waiting for more explanation. I didn't give him one. I wouldn't have known how. I closed my door, but I didn't put enough strength into the motion and the door just bounced against the catch.

"Didn't close," said Lucas, and he leaned way over to reach across my lap, grabbed the handle, and jerked the door shut with a slam. The brush of his arm set off so many thoughts in my head I could hardly breathe. Lucas took my seat belt while he was leaning over and fastened it around me.

"Thank you," I said.

"Any time."

I waited for him to start the engine, but he didn't. "Something wrong?" I said.

"Yes. I don't much want to head for home."

"A few days ago you seemed resigned to the farm."

"I sort of am. I even sort of like it. But I want other things more." He didn't look at me when he said that. He looked wistfully up at the campus spread on the mountainside.

"If this were television," he said, "I'd tell my parents they're crazy and I'd just leave. Stride down the dirt road to live happily ever after the way I chose."

"Television always ties up the loose ends so neatly, doesn't it? Kind of makes you jealous that you can't wrap up all your own problems between commercials."

He gave me a limp smile. "I didn't know you had problems, Marnie. You've seemed pretty

116

cheerful lately. Happy. I figured you settled into the routine and got to love it."

"I've settled into the routine, anyway. How could I not? There's so much to do, and if you don't do it right the first time, and do it efficiently, it's just there waiting for you, like a repeat nightmare."

"Too true."

We made a list of chores we hated. It was quite a list.

"Then you really aren't happy," he said. "It's odd. I used to look over at you doing some chore like making soap and you and your mother would be laughing away, and I'd think, maybe it is all worth it when they're so happy."

I wanted to laugh till I wept. I said, "You know that coverlet I wove?"

He nodded.

"I was so proud of that coverlet, Lucas. I made it all myself. Aunt Ellen did have to pull out a lot three times and start me over on the pattern, but still, I made it. And it looks good. And sometimes when we finish baking, and there are six sweet potato pies sitting cooling for Uncle Bob to drive over to the resort and I know that I did that and it's my money that's going to feed the animals this week — well, that's pretty nice. And when you go out for chores and it's chillier than you thought, and you come back in and put on the sweater that I knit, that's pretty nice, too. And when I load the Fisher stove for the night and I think that you and I split that wood, I feel cozier

117

than I would if I just turned up a thermostat in the apartment. I guess I'm happy about all that."

"Those are the good things," he said. "You know, I truly thought we'd never be able to do anything. So we'd read a few books. There's only so much you can learn from a guidebook. When we got to that farm and actually started doing it, I was sure we'd kill ourselves with those saws and axes and knives. I thought we'd get crushed beneath the trees we cut down. I thought the barn would fall in on us when we were trying to figure out how to shore up the hayloft. I thought the goat would bite me and I'd get rabies."

We were giggling by now, the very first time Lucas and I had ever really sat and laughed together.

"The reason mother and I laugh so much when we make soap is because we're both terrified we're going to burn our hands off with the lye, only she won't admit it, and so we have these nervous explosions of giggles whenever we get near the pot."

"Remember when you put the nail through my hand? I kept praying I'd get some terrible infection from it and have to stay in the hospital for weeks and weeks, eating food off trays, basking under an electric blanket, reading armloads of library books, being hovered over by pink ladies."

"Using a real bathroom."

"Most of all, using a real bathroom." We grinned at each other, and Lucas sobered up. "But we learned how to do most of it, Marnie.

And every time I do something, whether it's finding an egg one of my hens has laid, or building that greenhouse, I have this feeling of wonder — sort of, well, almost joy — that I, bookworm Peterson, can actually manage this stuff."

"Not only manage," I said. "Do it as well as most people we could hire. Back home I couldn't scramble an egg. Now I'm half supporting us with my baking."

We began listing the things we liked about the farm and, surprisingly, that was quite a list, too. The birds who came to our feeders and sang from our trees. The crisp apples fresh from our own trees. The warmth of the stove on a winter morning. The calm pleasure of two fathers whose lives had been grim before. The scent of fresh-baked bread wafting out over the yard. The overwhelming appeal of newborn ducklings.

"But you're not happy, Marnie?" said Lucas again.

"It's too hard, Lucas. They've gone overboard. I don't want to put every ounce of my energy into being self-sufficient. A lot of it like the soap could be dropped without damaging the reasons we moved here. They've taken up everything at once, Lucas, and it's just too exhausting."

"Chinese interpreter say, Lady still yearn for flush toilet."

We laughed. "Oh, do I!" I said. "But one of my spring campaigns is to dress up that joint a little. I'm going to paint it, and add some pretty curtains, and buy a rug remnant for the floor, and

119

put on the wall that watercolor Connie did for me of her dogwoods."

Lucas began to laugh silently. His whole body laughed, trembling and quivering with amusement.

"What's so funny?" I demanded.

"Oh, Marnie, if I couldn't laugh at us I'd have gone crazy by now. I have this daydream, see, that I haul out every now and then and dust off. In this daydream I'm on a date. A real date. You know. With a girl and money and a car and a movie that we meant to watch, but didn't. And when we were in the mood for talking we'd talk about literature and life and truth and adulthood." Lucas shook his head, still laughing. "And here we are, you and I, talking about outhouses, the improvement thereof."

Did he mean this was the daydream? A real date, and I was it? Or did he mean he still had the daydream, and neither Marnie nor outhouses, the improvement thereof, qualified.

"I dream about dating, too," I said, keeping my voice even, seeing where the subject led us.

"I'll bet. You were ready to take the high school by storm when we left home. You still miss Joel?"

I hadn't even thought about Joel in so long that his name surprised me. "No," I said. "There wasn't much there, you know. A walk home. One kiss."

"No kidding. But you always come home from school demanding to know what the mail was. I thought what mattered to you most was hearing from Joel."

"He only wrote one postcard. And that wasn't very enthusiastic. He found another girlfriend right away."

"I'm sorry," said Lucas. He took my hand in a comforting gesture. I would have liked it better if he hadn't sounded genuinely sorry. A boy who really thinks it's too bad you lost your boyfriend probably doesn't yearn for you as his own girlfriend.

"How come you always leave me to walk alone?" I said, the words spilling out before I could realize what I was saying. "Why don't you ever wait for me when we get off the school bus so we can walk up the lane together?"

Lucas was totally astonished. "I'm sorry again," he said. "I didn't know that bothered you. I mean, you often have something pretty cutting to say to me. I figured you needed a rest from my company. We do see kind of a lot of each other."

I'd rather see more of you than of the barnyard, I thought. More of you and less of sweet potato pie. "I didn't mean all those nasty cracks," I said. He looked skeptical. "Well, I did mean them, back when I said them," I admitted. Lucas looked back up at the college campus. "But I'm sorry for them now, Lucas. I just want to be friends, okay? I — I retract every insult I ever dished out."

Lucas smiled at me, his usual nice courteous smile. The one he directed equally at teachers, his mother, the geese, and me. "I guess I tossed out a few insults, too. It's okay. Forget it."

We were silent for a while.

"There are a few hours left before we need to

head home," said Lucas. "You want to go buy that paint? Or drive around and see what other stores there are? Or go to that amusement park, or what?"

I took a plunge. "Is this a date?" I said. "Or just a ploy to stay off the farm for a while?"

Lucas grinned. "It's just a ploy to — "

I felt tears coming into my eyes. Lucas broke off. When I finally looked at him, the silence had filled the car to the point of suffocation. We were as separated in our seats and seatbelts as if we'd been on opposite sides of a classroom during college boards.

"It's a date," said Lucas.

Chapter XII

"Tweetsie Railroad," said Lucas, turning into the parking lot. "You'd sure think they could have come up with a less ridiculous name than that."

"Oh, I don't know. I kind of picture a tiny yellow engine with a little plinking motor, pulling miniature cars up a steep mountainside."

"Sounds like Switzerland. Probably the meadows will be dotted with goats."

"No, please," I said, "anything but goats!"

We pulled a tarp over our purchases and locked the VW carefully. "Although potential thieves of manure forks are probably few and far between," said Lucas. We climbed steep stairs, bought tickets, and went up more stairs to a wide, graveled area, featuring old-time stores, pretend horses tied to the rails with real kids riding them, and at the station, about to leave, the train.

"I guess it isn't miniature," said Lucas.

"Doesn't seem to be yellow, either," I said. It was a big, black steam engine, pulling several handsome cars. The engineer pulled its whistle and the air was filled with a huge whooshing TOOOOT that was as romantic to me as a sliver of silver airplane in the sky — a sort of carefree gypsy sound. "You can just feel yourself going somewhere," murmured Lucas. We watched the train pull out. There weren't many passengers, and all of them were crowded into the last car, which was the only one with glassed-in sides. I couldn't understand why they didn't like the open cars. The train chugged off.

"I wouldn't normally think of a train as pretty," said Lucas, "but Tweetsie Railroad is definitely pretty."

We crossed the tracks and walked up a steep asphalt path to a large building with an open-sided snack bar. "Oh, good," said Lucas, "I'm starved. You know, I was sure your mother would pack some enormous picnic basket for us to take along, so we'd have plenty of good, solid, nutritious food, and wouldn't be tempted to waste precious quarters on greasy, junky, store-bought food. You could have knocked me over with goose down when she handed me a twenty-dollar bill and told me to buy whatever meals we needed. Why'd she do that?"

Because this is a date that she arranged, I thought, and as you just reminded me, a real date includes money, a car, and a girl. For someone who is supposed to be such a whiz at adding things up, your track record is kind of poor, Lucas. I said, "I guess to give us a treat."

"It sure is a treat." He got each of us a little tray of French fries and a small Coke.

Down in Boone the wind had merely been brisk, an energetic, rather companionable, wind. Here it whipped through my jacket as if I were clad in a bikini. It was so cold it hurt. No wonder the train's passengers rode in the enclosed car!

We tried a little round table in the back of the snack area, but the wind seemed to be having a convention in that corner.

We tried a ledge outside the snack bar where the sun shone, but the sun was no match for that wind.

Finally Lucas found a little pocket between two huge planters. We sat on the ground and let the wind whistle over us. Between wind whistles was the intermittent TOOOOT of the train now on the other side of the mountain. "I'm freezing," I whispered.

"You don't have to keep it a secret. I'm sure everybody else is, too."

"I'm also not very comfortable."

Lucas sprawled himself a bit more, his back against the row of railroad ties that formed the planter. "Here. Sit in my lap. Body heat, you know. Very good source of heat. Free. Requires no splitting, cutting, or hauling."

So I sat in his lap, and Lucas opened his coat buttons and when I leaned back against his chest he partly wrapped me in his coat as well as my own. It required considerable dexterity to drink our Cokes from this position, but I had no complaints and if Lucas did he didn't mention them.

Those French fries — the first I'd had in over a year — were hot, salty, greasy, and absolutely yummy.

"I can't decide why they're so good," said Lucas. "Do you think it's just that we haven't had them in so long? That all the wholesome food we've been eating left our tastebuds wide open to the seduction of real honest junk food?"

"Don't you wish," I said, referring to the position more than to the cuisine, "that we could eat like this every day?"

Lucas assumed I meant the French fries. "No, actually, I don't. I used to have such a rotten complexion, Marnie. I only liked my face from the eyebrows up, because my forehead was smooth. I used to keep my face in a book all the time because then all you could see of me was my handsome forehead."

"You do have a nice forehead."

"Thank you. I can't prove it was the food, but my face cleared up when we got to the farm."

"I'll eat your French fries for you, then."

"Oh, no, you don't. When I'm on a junk food binge I don't share with anybody. In fact, I think I'll buy us another round to eat on the train."

We got the food, but the train wouldn't go out again for another half hour so Lucas decided we should take the chairlift up the mountain. I decided I should stay at the bottom and wait for him.

"Chicken," said Lucas.

"I am not. If there's one thing I've found out about chickens, it's that they're dumb enough to do anything. Even ride on a chairlift."

"Come on, hop in, it's perfectly safe."

I held back. The attendant yawned. "It is safe, Miss," he said, bored. "You won't . . . well, okay, you missed that chair, we'll put you on the next one, they don't stop for more than a second, so you . . . well, you missed that one, too, the people behind you in line are starting to get a little edgy, Miss, if you could just — "

"Marnie, get in," said Lucas, shoving, and I was in. "What are you afraid of? This isn't more than fifteen feet off the ground."

"It's flimsy."

"It's a very thick cable."

"Looks like string to me."

The attendant slammed a tiny, thin, useless bar across our laps and the lift jerked and we flounced several feet forward. There was another jerk while the next passenger got on and another flounce forward. "Let's not do this," I said.

"I think they probably frown on people vaulting out of the chairlift, Marnie. Sit tight. Nothing will happen."

"I should have taken out life insurance."

"Even if you did fall, it's just a little way to the ground."

"That isn't ground down there, Lucas, those are the lethal tips of trees eager to impale me."

Lucas laughed, shifting over next to me. The lift now quivered left and right, as well as front and back. I squealed. The wind, which had merely been fierce on the ground, tore around us with the brutality of a young hurricane. "And this is April," I moaned. "What's it like in January?"

"I am beginning to think you are not cut out to be, say, a ski instructor, Marnie."

"Lucas, I am *freezing!*"

Lucas pulled me next to him, something I'd have cooperated with if I hadn't been sure than any movement would tip us both out, and wrapped my left side with his arm. I closed my eyes, pressed my face into his chest, and listened to his heart-beat. Lucas took advantage of my cowardice to remove my French fries from my death grip. He ate them as calmly as if we were in a cafeteria. "Marnie!" he yelled over the wind.

"What?" I muttered through the thick wool of his sweater. My sweater, which I had knit for him.

"Relax! Enjoy yourself!" shouted Lucas.

"I am, I am."

And I was.

I was freezing. My legs were cold, my cheeks were cold, my neck was cold, even the fillings in my teeth were cold. I knew the lift would break the next time the cable twitched and we'd both go to gory deaths on some spiky trees.

And tucked under Lucas' arm, listening to his heart, I was having the most wonderful time of my life.

I was actually sorry when we had to get off the lift at the top of the mountain. Getting off turned out to be much easier than getting on. More incentive, I guess.

We toured an old mine shaft. Lucas would comment on this or that and I would go "mmmm" or "aaah," but all I was aware of was that my left hand was getting frostbite and my right hand was snuggled in Lucas'. He had taken the hand all on his own. I hadn't offered it or anything. "So how do we get down?" I said at last, watching the floucing chairlift from a nice, safe distance.

"There's a minibus for people who are afraid of chairlifts," he said. I felt a deep gratitude for the Tweetsie Railroad managers, who had known this sort of thing would come up from time to time.

The instant the minibus drew to its stop, we saw the train below us getting ready once more to pull out. "Wait for us!" screamed Lucas. I personally did not feel such an urgent need to catch the train, but Lucas didn't let go of my hand, and rather than have my arm jerked out its socket, I ran with him. We tore down the steep paths and across the tracks right in front of the train. "It won't leave when we're in its way," explained Lucas. "They hardly ever like to kill the customers." We leaped on the first passenger car and wilted against its sides, panting and huffing. The train gave a final TOOOOT and pulled slowly and noisily out of the station.

"There's a glassed-in car at the rear," said the ticket officer. "Everybody else is down there to keep out of the wind."

"We're tough," said Lucas. "A little wind doesn't bother us."

"Bothers me," I said, still trying to catch my breath.

"I've always wanted a train car all to myself," said Lucas. "This is one very minor childhood fantasy come true."

"Don't have it to yourself," observed the ticket officer. "There's a girl with you."

"Another fantasy," said Lucas, and both he and the ticket man grinned.

We both wanted a window seat, but I certainly didn't want to sit in a different row from Lucas, so I sat next to him. The train curved around the mountainside. In places the trees closed around us, dense and green with new spring leaves. In others were vistas over wide meadows to the pretty little valley below.

"Marnie," said Lucas.

"Yes?"

"What did we decide this is?"

"I'm pretty sure it's a train, Lucas."

"No, no. This afternoon."

I drew a blank. I didn't know what he meant.

"A ploy to stay off the farm," said Lucas, "or a date?"

There was no train, no wind, no people, no scenery then. Just looking at each other, and trying to decide what to say, what to think. I decided that since speech was often a short-coming between us, I'd forget it. I sat in Lucas' lap again, and handsome as his forehead might be, that wasn't where I kissed him.

"I guess it's a date then," said Lucas when we stopped to breathe.

We laughed and stopped the laughter with more kisses. It wasn't like junior high. We didn't miss. We didn't get each other's chins damp or feel silly. It was warm, soft and —

"KKIIIIIYYYYY-YIIIIIYYYYY-YIIIIIYY-YYY!!!"

Huge, whooping screams filled the air. I was so startled I leaped out of Lucas' grip, found myself half standing, half crouching, hanging onto the seat back, and staring into the leering eyes of a masked horseman who had drawn up next to our railroad car. Men on horses dashed back and forth, screaming, yelling, and shooting. I was paralyzed.

"That'll teach you to kiss," said Lucas, laughing so hard he choked. "They caught you. You won't do that again in a hurry, will you?"

"Lucas, what is this?"

"It's a game. Everybody in school has been here a dozen times. Didn't any of them ever tell you what happens when you ride Tweetsie Railroad?"

"No. I thought you just rode around the mountain."

"You do. You also get robbed. Every time the train goes out, bad guys hold up the good guys. Those are college kids making a little money screeching and shooting and riding horses."

I was so embarrassed I could have died. Every one of those riders knew they had really terrified me. Where their mouths showed under their masks, they were laughing, congregating around our car. I flopped into the seat beside Lucas and shrank down out of view.

"Don't worry about it," said Lucas. "Your mind was on other things."

"And yours wasn't?"

"I was a little distracted. But I knew it was coming."

"Do they actually rob us? I'm a little short on gold. They'll have to settle for the cherrywood bracelet your father carved for me."

"I wonder if they need any more robbers," mused Lucas. "I can't ride a horse, but if I can learn how to farm, I guess I can learn that. Sounds like a much easier way to earn money that sweet potato pie making."

I just slumped, letting my pulse slow down, and hoping my cheeks weren't permanently blushed. Lucas slumped down to match my position. There can't be anything more awkward than being half on a floor, half on a hard, wooden bench, wind whistling through your hair, gunshots going over your head. It turned out, however, to be a very acceptable position for another kiss. And another, and another.

I knew for sure that Lucas no longer put me in the sister category.

What I still didn't know was if, given a selection, Marnie MacDonald was the girl he'd have chosen to date.

Chapter XIII

My loft had never been cozier. I snuggled into my quilt. Before she went to bed Mother had opened the windows and cool, spring, night air drifted in. I fell asleep thinking of Lucas and love and how perhaps our parents were right — this *was* the good life! Except for them, the good part would be farming, and for me the good part would be Lucas.

We'd paint his room together. Laughing. Enjoying it. Making it attractive. We'd build his shelves and drawers together. One of these days he'd ask me for a real date. He'd think of some way to find a few dollars (or at least a few hours) and arrange for the two of us to be alone, somewhere, somehow.

When I woke up, my mother was calling my name over and over. "It's late, Marnie. You'll miss the bus. Hurry and dress. I've got a sweet roll for you to eat while you rush down the lane."

So much for a leisurely breakfast with a single rose at my place and an atmosphere redolent of romance. The only thing our house was redolent of was scurrying sounds of six people getting ready to leave it.

I dressed as quickly as I could, backing down my ladder without getting a run in my stockings. I stood over the kitchen table, gulping my apple juice (one of the things I yearn for most is frozen orange juice; I grew up believing Vitamin C came only in frozen orange juice and it's very hard to believe my own squashed apples will also keep my body functioning), and my father said, "The last possible frost date has gone by, Marnie. Forecast for the rest of the week is in the seventies. This breeze is drying out the soil and everything is just perfect for planting our summer crops. Beans, corn, squash, tomatoes, and so on."

"That's nice," I said. I stacked my books, looking for Lucas. I had heard him earlier, but he didn't seem to be in the house now.

"So the minute you get home from school, get into your jeans, and meet us in the garden to get working. We want to get everything done now. Forecast for the weekend is heavy rain, which will be good for the new seeds, assuming it isn't too heavy, of course, in which case . . ." He tapered off into a monologue about the vagaries of weather and the precarious position of the farmer.

That wasn't nice. It meant instead of a date with Lucas, I had a date with a garden. Oh, well. Lucas and I could stoop over the same carrot row. It wasn't a rose on a lace-covered tray, but at least it was proximity.

I hurried outdoors. It was warm, and the breeze

was soft, full of flowery scents. Sometimes I wish I had a strong nose, like an animal, so I could identify everything, and know where it came from, and when, instead of just getting a faint, mish-mashy perfume.

Lucas was just coming out of the barn. He must have had to check on the cow or the goats. He brushed himself off, picked up his bookbag from the porch step, and we headed for the bus stop.

"I've got an exam," said Lucas. "I should have studied yesterday instead of running all over the place."

He would rather have been studying than driving me around Boone? Would rather have been studying than giving me kisses, talking to me about Life, Truth, and Outhouses, the improvement thereof?

"Sorry," he said. "Didn't meant to hurt your feelings. That's usually your scene, isn't it?"

"What do you mean?"

"A few verbal stabs just when I don't need them."

"Lucas, I told you yesterday how sorry I am for all that."

"Yeah, you did."

The bus came. Our conversation — if you could call it that — ended, because Lucas didn't try to sit with me, even though there were plenty of empty seats. He fell into a seat beside one of the boys and immediately opened a book to begin studying. I ended up with Eloise, Connie, apparently sick again, showing Eloise how to do remainders on long division.

It wasn't what I had had in mind for today at all.

It was impossible to keep my mind on class. I kept running through those few little sentences, as if I were in a play and had to have them by memory. What had Lucas meant by that? Was he telling me he couldn't forgive me for all the mean things I'd said? Was he telling me to buzz off, because studying had a much higher priority than I did? Or was he just nervous about an exam he hadn't prepared for, and the stress made him unaware of what he was saying to me?

When my teachers called on me, I didn't know what page we were on or what the topic was, and once, I wasn't even sure which class I was in. I don't know who was annoyed more, the teachers or me.

Coming home I got on the bus early. Lucas will be in a good mood, I told myself. The test will have been easy, because tests are always easy for Lucas, and the sun is shining, and life is good, and we'll be friends.

Lucas emerged from the building at the last possible second and ran to catch the bus, leaping onto the moving steps just as it pulled out. He didn't so much as glance at any of us, but squatted beside the folding exit doors to talk to the bus driver.

"Don't worry about it, Marnie," said Eloise, patting my hand.

"Don't worry about what?"

"Lucas."

"What makes you think I am worried about Lucas?"

"All you ever do is make cow eyes at him. Do you know that you did one of my division problems wrong, and the teacher made me do it on the board, and I didn't know how? All because you are dotty about Lucas."

"I am not dotty about anyone and I have never made cow eyes in my life."

"Connie says you have a crush on him."

I had never said that to Connie. Suddenly I wondered just how much everybody did know. Was it painfully obvious that I loved Lucas and he had no use for me? Did every single person on this bus know that I had been hoping Lucas would sit with me and been in pain when he didn't?

I was quite glad when our bus stop came. I was afraid Eloise would tell me that she had never seen Lucas make cow eyes at me so he must not have a crush the way I did. I was afraid Eloise would tell me that when I wasn't looking, Lucas was making cow eyes at someone else.

Cow eyes, I thought, gathering my books. What a revolting phrase.

Although cows do have beautiful eyes. Large, amazed, dumb, brown eyes. Was that what I looked like when I faced Lucas?

Lucas was off the bus first, of course, since he was perched on the steps, and by the time I got off he was already a hundred feet down the lane, swinging along, whistling to himself.

It was the whistling that hurt most. Such a

137

carefree sound. Happiness with pursed lips. A boy alone on a country lane, enjoying himself.

My insides ached.

I pretended to drop my books, so as the bus pulled away anyone watching would have thought it perfectly normal for me to stand by the roadside stooping and gathering them up. It surprised me somewhat that I cared what they thought. I'd have said that if Lucas didn't care, then nobody mattered at all. But apparently I didn't really feel that way. Maybe somehow I needed a reason even for myself for the distance between Lucas and me.

The sun was no longer a friendly, warm yellow. It was a hot hammer, whacking the insides of my head until it throbbed.

Okay, Lucas, I thought, if that's the way you want it, so be it. You couldn't be making it more plain that you didn't intend our trip to turn out the way it did. Any kisses exchanged were meaningless, and no conclusions should be drawn from the conversations.

I accept that, I told myself. Look at me shrug.

I even shrugged. It was a shoulder movement, though. It didn't have a whole lot to do with me. *I* wasn't shrugging at all.

It's probably just as well, I said to myself. Living together the way we do, it could be awkward for us to be in love. My bedroom in the loft, his a few feet away behind the kitchen. A mild friendship, that's probably much more healthy.

Who cares? I don't care.

Beside me was the thick hedgerow that ran

along Mr. Shields' property. He had dozens and dozens of forsythia bushes, which four weeks earlier had been a gaudy ribbon of gold. This week all the gold was gone and the bushes were a bright new green. In the middle of all this was a slender weedy renegade, just now coming out with blossoms peeking through all that green. I felt a tremendous affection for that bush. Setting my books down in the rutted lane, I began slowly picking forsythia branches.

I'm not going to cry, I told myself. Lucas is not worth one single salty tear.

I had to do deep-breathing exercises to keep from crying, because the other half of me was saying, Lucas is worth a million salty tears! Cry, flood the lousy lane, get your eyes red, scream even.

I picked forsythia instead.

"Marnie?" said Lucas. His softest voice. Nothing at all resembling a newborn foghorn. A deep, gentle baritone.

"I'll carry your books for you," he said.

I had not even heard him walk up to me. I kept my eyes on my armload of flowers, making myself think which vase I'd put them in. The narrow-topped, dark-brown pottery, or the thick crystal vase that Mother hadn't, after all, given to the yard sale? "Thought you were already hard at work in the garden," I said.

"I should be."

We both should be, I thought drearily. The word garden is so pretty. Why isn't the work involved pretty, too?

"Marnie, wait, please."

"I'm walking beside you, Lucas, what is there to wait for?" There. I had snapped at him again. What a habit it was for me, really. No wonder he liked to walk alone.

"I'm sorry," he said unexpectedly. "You told me you didn't like it when I walked on ahead and I did it anyhow. On purpose."

At least he admitted it. But I wasn't too thrilled he came back out of guilt for his bad manners. The last thing I wanted was Lucas around because he had been brought up to be courteous. I wanted him around because he couldn't bear to be anywhere else. "Doesn't matter," I said.

"You remember yesterday?"

I almost said, "Certainly I remember yesterday, you think I'm senile?" But I caught it in time and merely answered, "Yes."

He took my arm to stop me from walking farther. "Are you glad about it or sorry?"

"I'm glad it happened yesterday, Lucas. I'm sorry it's not happening today."

There, I'd done it. Said what I really felt, at the right time, with the right person. No flip nastiness about it. It made it possible for me to look at Lucas without the fear that I'd burst into tears, which neither of us needed.

Lucas looked awkward and upset. I could identify with that. He flushed when our eyes met and whatever it was he'd meant to say didn't come out. He muttered something about my flowers. Then he heaved a big sigh, turning me by the shoulders so he could look at me without

140

having to squint into the sun behind my back. "I rehearsed for this," he said. "Now I can't remember my lines."

"Sounds familiar," I said wryly. "Give me a hint and I'll give you a cue."

"Sometimes I hate speech, Marnie. I read somewhere that deaf and dumb married people never get divorced. Experts think it's because they never exchange words. I always sort of hope I'll get things across with ESP, or something, but I never do, and I'm stuck with words."

"I know what you mean. Lots of times I want to say something, but I don't know how, and then I think, how crazy, I've been speaking for seventeen years, of *course* I know how."

Lucas grinned. "It's so odd, Marnie. Every time you say something I think, that's just it, that's just how I feel. And then I think, Marnie and I feel the same way about something? Impossible."

"I guess . . . I guess we've both changed a lot in the last year, Lucas."

"You certainly have. You're incredibly different. I . . . I know I wasn't nice on the bus. I did that on purpose. I just don't know what to think about . . . about liking you so much. It feels so strange. Yesterday . . . it was . . . well, it was terrific, and in the morning, I thought, with Marnie, who thinks the only thing I can do is walk on the bottoms of my feet, I had this terrific time?"

"Lucas, I've been wanting to do something with you for so long! You were always feeding the goats or something. Yesterday was terrific for me,

141

too. And I retract a million times over the bit about the bottoms of your feet. Okay?"

We looked at each other. There were an awful lot of flowers and books between us. After a while we set them all down and stood in the middle of the lane and kissed.

"Say," said Mr. Shields, "I like that. Decorates the old lane a lot better than the scarecrow my wife usually puts up."

We jumped apart and Mr. Shields laughed. "Going to be any repeat performances?" he wanted to know.

"I apologize," I said, "we didn't mean to annoy you or anything. We just —"

"Marnie, m'dear, the only thing annoying me is that I've smoked so many cigarettes for so long I couldn't possibly sustain a kiss as long as you two did. I felt like applauding."

Very slowly, Lucas and I walked the rest of the way home. Lucas felt it was only neighborly to give Mr. Shields a few repeat performances.

Chapter XIV

"Marnie! Lucas! Stop wasting time. We need you."

We were separated: me to the kitchen garden to set out strawberry plants, Lucas to the far field to finish the cultivating.

We waved at each other a few times, but we didn't have a moment together until dinner, which came very late, since we worked outdoors until dusk.

For the first time I noticed that at dinner we seemed to have assigned seats. Aunt Ellen, Uncle Bob, and Lucas always sat on the window side of the trestle table. We MacDonalds invariably sat on the opposite side, starting with me across from Aunt Ellen, Mother across from Uncle Bob, and Dad across from Lucas. We need a new arrangement here, I thought, but by the time I knew I wanted to sit next to Lucas for a change, or at least across from him, everybody else had sagged to a seat and the only empty chair left was my usual one.

There was no chance to talk during dinner. Our parents monopolized the conversation, comparing notes over what had been accomplished.

As for after dinner, Lucas had a book report to write, and I had an English exam, and both of us would have been tempted to skip them in favor of a good night's sleep, so we found our mothers monitoring us.

The following morning I managed to get myself awake earlier than usual, so I could have a leisurely breakfast with Lucas. It was warm, and dressing, I thought, maybe we can eat on the porch. Just us.

But it turned out Lucas had been up since three A.M. with a sick goat and the vet had finally arrived so Lucas could get out of the barn. He was awake, but staggered silently down the lane to get the school bus and slept all the way to school.

Actually, I didn't mind. I had never watched Lucas sleep before, and it was a surprisingly satisfactory thing to observe. Connie kept up a steady chatter next to me and didn't appear to notice that I never looked her way. Getting off the bus, though, Connie said, "By the way, Marnie . . ."

"Mmmmm?"

"Julie and I wanted to know if the handholding situation between you and Lucas is still at the reaching for chicken eggs level."

I giggled. "No. I think we've progressed beyond that."

"Julie will be disappointed. But I'm not. I think it's neat."

I thought it was rather neat myself.

Connie carefully located Eloise for the bus ride home, which Lucas barely managed to notice, his eyes were so close to sleep again. "I'd ask you for a date, Marnie," he yawned, "if I weren't sleepy, busy, broke, and all that sort of thing."

"It's the thought that counts."

"My mother likes to say that. I disagree. Thinking about a date doesn't make it a date, and a real-life date is a lot better than counting up your thoughts about dating."

"Right on."

He slept the rest of the way home. We'd have dawdled in the lane (for Mr. Shields' sake, of course), but Uncle Bob happened to be plowing a field near the bus stop and gave us our marching orders. Or, in our case, planting orders.

It seemed the weather forecast had changed. Rain was expected with slightly lower temperatures and we had to finish getting the seeds in today.

And when I'd finished my share of five, solid, backbreaking hours of raking, marking, sowing, and tamping the garden, the only thing I was good for was a cup of soup and bed.

It came to me that in order to be a success at dating, the money, the car, the movie tickets and all that weren't nearly so important as *time*.

145

Everybody I knew had time to lounge around, to joke, get a soda, dawdle, sit around.

Everybody except Lucas and me.

It seemed the final blow in a year that included an awful lot of blows. I had survived the transplant to the country, fallen in love, gotten to the point where Lucas actually admitted to liking me back, only to find there wasn't time for love.

It wasn't love yet, except on my part. Lucas was still getting used to the mere idea of liking me. We'd exchanged — what? — a dozen kisses. We had a long way to go!

We need time! I'd think desperately.

But I never found much.

I actually ached for Lucas. I'd always thought that was a book-type exaggeration, but it's true. You can want to hug somebody so much your arms ache.

Sometimes in the evening when we slumped around listening to the radio news before bedtime, I'd see Lucas looking at me. Now and then we'd go for short walks, looking for a little seclusion, a little time.

A little was just what we got, too. Five minutes here, two minutes there.

Lucas and I developed a hand signal. We'd rotate our thumbs at each other whenever our parents' enthusiasm became more than we could stand. It meant that for two cents we'd hitchhike to New York and leave them to their farm. Like the time Lucas' father decided to get a horse and buggy and sell the VW bus. Fortunately Mother and Aunt Ellen scotched that one, pointing out we had to be able to get our baked things to the resort. "You could do it with a horse and buggy," grumbled Uncle Bob.

"Yes, we could," said Mother, "but the resort likes its pies fresh."

Everybody laughed.

Lucas said, "I thought I'd run into town with Marnie today. I have to get a few things."

"Just give me your list," said Aunt Ellen. "I have to go anyway, and we certainly don't want to waste the gasoline on two separate trips."

"You know," said my father, "I ought to teach Marnie how to drive. She's sixteen now and — "

"Seventeen," I said.

"You're seventeen?" said my father. "Time flies when you're having fun, doesn't it?"

"I'll teach her how to drive," said Lucas.

"No, Lucas, the mower attachment for the tractor is acting up and you're the most mechanical. You need to be working on that."

"It'll only take me a few hours," said Lucas. "Then I can teach Marnie."

"A parent," my father informed us, "should not be continually foisting his parental duties off on others."

"Foist, foist," I said, but my father turned out to be my driving teacher.

I tried to take a long time learning how to drive, so that Lucas would have to take me out at least once. I had visions of finding a country lane so narrow with such deep ditches that once I drove in there would be no getting out, and Lucas and I would just have to sit in the car for ages and ages.

Unfortunately I proved to be a very quick driving student. I had had to drive the VW quite a lot in first gear or reverse, what with hauling stuff between house and barn, or getting the van out of somebody's way, and, of course, I could drive the tractor. What with that (and probably, said my father with immense satisfaction, lots of innate ability), I was driving like a pro at the end of two afternoons of trying. Dad wanted me to take the drivers' test the very next day. I insisted on more practice. My father insisted on practicing with me. "Lucas could," I said.

"Marnie, I've been driving for twenty-five years. Lucas has been driving for two. Now, who would make the better teacher?"

Lucas, definitely Lucas.

But it was always my father. I got my license and immediately I became errand-runner-in-chief. Taking pies, bread, and cakes to the resort. Getting feed at FCX, and yeast and salt at the grocery, and tools at the Sears pick-up. Taking rhubarb to the Farmers' Market, goats' milk to the natural foods store, paying bills, asking the county agent for a pamphlet on yet another project my parents wanted to investigate.

Lucas graduated from Valley High, but missed the ceremony.

The apple trees developed blight and the agricultural agent told us if we intended to save our crop we'd have to spray on a regular systematic basis. The thought of using chemicals tore our parents up, but in the end there was no choice. It was spray or lose everything.

The day of graduation, Lucas was spraying apple trees. "Somehow," he said to me, strapping on his mask and gear, "this isn't what I had in mind to celebrate my diploma."

Lucas kept his chin up, considering how depressed he was. His best friends both at Valley and back home were getting ready for college. Planning wardrobes, earning spending money, memorizing catalog offerings, writing to future roommates, wondering about majors and minors. And he, Lucas Peterson, of the debate team, literary magazine, and honor roll — he wasn't going.

That summer, incredibly, was even more exhausting than the first. So many things had been started and now it seemed imperative to our parents not only to finish each project, but also to succeed in them.

"I believe in hitching your wagon to a star," said Lucas, "but just one star at a time, not the whole damn galaxy."

The amount of work was overwhelming.

The amount of time Lucas and I could spend together was underwhelming. Like zero.

Still, there were good moments.

Lucas collapsed with exhaustion after unloading fifty hundred-pound bags of lime from the delivery truck and sat folded over on a stack of three lime bags. "Do sit with me," he said, his voice coming up from between his knees where his head was

149

hanging. "I have this lovely seat at the opera here. They're doing *Madame Butterfly*. Won't you join me?"

"Partying again?" I said. "Really, Lucas. You playboys."

"Too much high living," he said. "Going to my head."

And there was the lady from Boston who had heard we kept geese, and wanted a supply of empty goose eggs to decorate for her Christmas tree. She was obviously a little leery of associating with such filthy hicks as Lucas and me. I guess we looked like a cartoon strip to her, complete with overalls, scarves on my hair, cap on Lucas', and Lucas had recently taken up chewing long grasses, which perpetually hung out of his mouth. We had eleven goose eggs we could give her, but I tripped coming down the porch steps and she only got two goose eggs for all her trouble.

"Let's go to California," I said to Lucas, as he washed the scrapes on my knees.

"I hear they hire a lot of migrant labor out there," he said. "We could set up house in the VW van and follow the crops all over the West."

I would have scraped my knees open daily for the privilege of Lucas kneeling beside me and worrying about my skin.

"Actually," he said, "I've chartered a yacht for the week. Shall we sail to Bermuda?"

"No. Let's just sit here and watch the traffic go by."

The lady from Boston was trying to back out of our driveway. It really was rather entertaining, until the lives of our animals were in danger. Lucas drove it out for her, but she lined the seat with newspaper first so he wouldn't ruin it.

"Six P.M.," said Lucas. "Bedtime."

"Early to bed, early to rise, makes a man healthy, wealthy, and wise."

"The health I can see. The wealth is proving a bit elusive. And as for wisdom I'm really not sure. We may be featuring it and we may not."

"The lady from Boston definitely feels we're not."

One rainy day my mother was sewing, Aunt Ellen was weaving, Uncle Bob was at the vets' conferring about something or other, and my father was trying to build a goat stanchion. Lucas and I had been assigned the task of caulking the windows so that next winter the wind's roar would be down to a whistle as it passed through our walls.

The stuff was a quick-drying foam insulation that came in a rather small tube, but upon emerging became puffy and bloated, thus filling up your cracks quite well. By now, of course, Lucas and I were quite sure we knew how to do everything, so we didn't bother to read the directions. We moved from window to window, making quips about possible dates, kissing whenever we were out of the view of a parent, and generally enjoying ourselves. It took about two hours.

"Whew!" said Lucas, throwing away the empty tubes of foam. "Now let's wash this muck off. It's all over my hands."

It was all over mine, too. Thick, scabby-looking

white stuff, faintly resembling cement. We went outdoors to the pump and pumped water over each others' hands.

The stuff didn't come off.

We tried soap. We tried cleansers. We tried sand. We even tried steel wool and tweezers and a knife blade.

It didn't come off.

We looked at each other in horror mixed with hysterical laughter. I retrieved the foam tubes from the trash. "Apply only when wearing gloves," I read. "Do not get on skin. Forms immediate permanent bond."

I stared down at my hands. They looked infested.

It was not possible to hide the hands from our parents. We got all the usual, "Why didn't you follow the directions? Why don't you ever listen? What's the matter with you?" stuff. But none of it cleaned our hands.

It took five days for the stuff to wear off. My hands were sore and tender for weeks afterward. But it had its good points. Lucas and I had a very good reason to sit quietly in the dark, rubbing lotion into each other's hands, and although I wouldn't do the same thing the next time I caulk a window, it was sort of — almost — worthwhile.

"You'll never guess what I found growing over in the damp place by the woods," said Aunt Ellen. "Where that underground spring is."

"No, what?" I said. If it was more work, I

152

hoped it would just fade back into the woods from whence it came.

"Blueberries. About a dozen high bush blueberries. Somebody must have planted them there years ago. They've become so thick and bushy and tall, and what's more, full of perfect, ripe berries. The birds have pecked a lot off the tops of the bushes, but we couldn't reach up there anyway. There's a tremendous amount just waiting for us."

My mother smiled at me. We hadn't talked much about Lucas and me partly because we were all so busy, but she knew how I felt, and had seen the change in Lucas. "I think Lucas and Marnie should spend the day picking blueberries," she said. "We've got plenty of pails. Let them take sandwiches and a thermos of lemonade and get us enough blueberries for the entire winter."

Nobody argued. Nobody mentioned eleven urgent chores requiring Lucas' expertise. Nobody listed essential errands for me to run.

Lucas hitched the small wagon to the tractor. My father filled it with pails, Mother put in the picnic basket, Lucas tossed in a blanket, and yelled for me to come on.

"A blanket?" said his father. "You're supposed to pick berries, not take naps."

"Marnie," said my mother.

"Yes, Mother?"

"That blanket."

"We aren't going to do anything, Mother."

"A boy, a girl, and a blanket? Don't be ridiculous, Marnie, of course you're going to do something. Just don't do very much, okay?"

I giggled. "This is supposed to be the free life, remember?"

"You're not *that* free."

"Mother, I don't even know if Lucas wants to do anything with me. For all I know he's bringing the blanket to spread the sandwiches on."

"No," said my mother. "He is not bringing the blanket for the sandwiches."

"Marnie!" yelled Lucas. "Hurry up. Those blueberries are growing old."

"And so am I, so am I," murmured my mother.

"Oh, Mother, stop worrying. You're the one who suggested it, anyhow. And no fair climbing the hill with binoculars."

"I'd never do a thing like that," she said indignantly. She hugged me suddenly, and kissed me, as if she were sending me off to college or war. Lucas yelled again and I ran to get in the wagon.

"For pete's sake, Marnie," said Lucas, "don't ride in the wagon."

"There's nowhere else to sit."

"My lap, my lap."

We bounced over the fields to the blueberry patch.

The sun was hot. There was no wind. After a while Lucas said, "Mind steering, Marnie?"

I steered. Lucas leaned back and stripped off his shirt. "Hot," he explained. I leaned back against him again, and decided that this ride was even better than the chairlift. Less between us. And no icy wind.

154

The blueberry bushes were right where Aunt Ellen had said they would be, and just as she had said, they were dripping with berries. And my father had put eighteen buckets in the wagon.

"Eighteen?" said Lucas faintly.

"Do they really expect us to fill eighteen buckets?" I said. "We won't be able to do anything except insanely heave berries into buckets from now until dark."

"Oh, were you thinking of doing anything besides picking blueberries?" said Lucas.

"I personally am not sufficiently fond of blueberries to spend an entire day of my life on them."

"Besides, a few blueberries go a long way. One handful for a whole mess of pancakes, and how often do we have pancakes?"

"Right."

We spread the blanket on the grass and spread ourselves on the blanket. After quite a long while Lucas mentioned that the blueberries did not seem to be filling the buckets on their own.

"Thoughtless of them," I said.

We lay on our backs and stared into the blue sky. "Our sky," said Lucas. "Our hill, our trees, our world."

"Our kiss."

"Do we really need city life when we can have all this, Marnie?"

"Yes!"

We laughed and kissed again.

"Nice," said Lucas.

"It would be nicer in the city."

"I'm sure a kiss is a kiss."

"Lucas, I'm feeling guilty."

"About what? Kisses? Marnie, you're a bona fide farm girl now. You know very well we haven't done anything to feel guilty about. Though if that's what you want, I'll be more than glad to — "

"No, guilty about not picking blueberries. They're all home, work, work, working and we're here — "

"Necking," said Lucas. "Isn't that a dumb word? I detest it."

"I think the neck is where you're supposed to stop."

"Let's not stop."

But we did stop, at the same moment, without speaking any more. It hurt to stop, like being wrenched by something invisible. Lucas worked the shady side of the bushes and I worked the sunny side. The blueberries annoyed me terribly. I had so many important things to think about — Lucas, for example — and there was always a goat or a parent or a blueberry between us.

Why had we stopped? I wasn't really sure. Pressure, almost, from parents who weren't there, and a duty to work we'd developed in the last year and a half. Maybe a little fear, too. That neither of us was ready for more than kissing.

The blueberries stopped plinking against the metal of my bucket, and landed softly on top of each other. I could have Lucas right now, I thought, and I chose blueberries. Weird.

"Marnie?" said Lucas through the leaves and the deep blue rounds of the berries.

"Yes?"

"I love you."

The words hung in the air, as if the sun's heat were rising from them. Lucas walked around the bushes, set his pail down, and looked at me, the edges of a grin beginning on his lips. He had said it first, not me. "I love you, Lucas."

Of course we'd have had a more successful embrace if I hadn't been holding my pail in front of me, but when it dropped the blueberries seemed of little importance.

"Your lips are blue," accused Lucas. "You've been eating more blueberries than you've picked."

"Your lips are normal. Didn't you eat a single one?"

"No."

"Allow me to feed you some of my number one, superior grade blueberries, then."

What with one thing and another when dusk came hours later, we each had but one pail of blueberries, and neither of those full.

Chapter XV

For two weeks both of us were in heaven. Glimpses of each other, touches, laughs, words — they were like a symphony. Two people being in love is a lot more fun than one person being in love.

And then school started.

I walked alone down the lane to catch the bus and sit with Connie, while Lucas worked in the barn or the orchards. School was hard. For the first time in my life I wanted excellent grades because for the first time I realized that if I were to go to college, it would have to be on a scholarship. B minus would not do. I had to have A's. And senior English, fourth year French, chemistry, and modern history were not an easy schedule. Between history and English I had weekly essays to write and a good deal of library research.

When Lucas was splitting wood, I was investigating English poets since World War One.

When Lucas was delivering the split wood at thirty-five dollars a load to townies, I was checking out volumes about the role of Palestine in modern turmoil.

When Lucas was rebuilding fences that had sagged over the summer, I was reading Balzac in French and composing letters to a pen pal in Marseilles for an exchange program.

When Lucas was unloading bushels of apples at the cider mill, getting splinters under his nails and tan on his bare shoulders, I was finding out what covalent and ionic bonds were.

Lucas did not want me to talk to him about school. He ached for school. My senior year; and the first year of his life since he was four years old that he had no school to go to. It would cause some people to rejoice. It hurt Lucas enough that it tainted all our conversations.

It wasn't like other high school romances. One of us wasn't in high school. Both of us had too much to do.

I wove my second coverlet and for Christmas knit my father and Uncle Bob pullovers. For Lucas I knit a beautiful vest, using the smallest needles I possessed. "Dressy," he said. "For wearing under a good suit."

"Keep it clean," I told him. "The time may come."

Lucas' solar greenhouse worked well. Nobody ever was as proud of anything as Lucas when he presented us with hand-pollinated tomatoes in mid-winter.

"Something just occurred to me," said Lucas.

"What is that?"

"We're not slaves."

I giggled. "No collar," I said, touching his throat. "No chains. I guess we're not."

"Seriously, Marnie. I'm eighteen, almost nineteen, and I'm doing as much work as anybody."

"That just occurred to you? I always knew that."

"Well, the conclusion to be drawn from those facts just occurred to me."

"Which is?"

"If I want to take the VW out one cold winter evening, and if I want to buy a movie ticket with my share of the split-wood income, and if I choose to ask you to go along with me, that is not only my privilege, it is my right. I do not, repeat *not,* require parental permission to do that."

It seemed incredible that we had never thought of it that way before. The adults told us we couldn't waste gas or spend money, so we didn't. But we *were* contributing — all *too* contributing — adult members of this household, and we did have a right to spend at least a little in whatever way *we* chose.

"You do, repeat *do,* have my permission to ask," I told Lucas.

"Marnie, would you like to go to the movies with me tonight after supper?"

"Why, Lucas, I'd love to. What an unusual idea. When can you pick me up?"

"Thought I'd drop by around seven."

160

"Make it six thirty, please. Around seven I'm scheduled to do dishes and I'd rather be gone."

"Nothing worse than dishpan hands." Lucas took my red hands in his calloused ones and we danced around the barn.

"I thought you hated dancing," I said.

"I never had a worthwhile partner before."

"Then let's go dancing."

"Where? Fantasy aside, the only dances I know of around here are those scheduled quarterly by the high school."

He was right. Darn! Why couldn't we live in a city? Why did we have to be stuck out here?

"Marnie, let's not even bother talking about that. Let's have a real date and talk about us."

Now there was a suggestion I could warm to.

After supper Lucas helped me clear the table and pour tea for everyone. But we didn't sit down. Lucas brought our coats and helped me into mine. "Marnie and I are going to the movies. We'll be back around eleven. See you."

"Lucas, it's such a waste of gas," said his mother. "And movie tickets are so expensive. There's a concert next month that would be worth going to see, worth saving up for, though."

"It isn't a waste of gas," said Lucas quietly. "Marnie and I need to get out once in a while."

"Everything you need is here," said his parents.

But everything we needed wasn't there. Nobody actually argued with us, but it was clear that our going out hurt them. Money aside, they truly felt that the farm should provide enough joy, that we shouldn't have to range away, go to a town for our fun.

We'd become very close, the six of us, working side by side, depending on each other for so much, from food to safety to warmth. It wasn't easy to do things that would hurt four of us for the sake of two of us. On my own, I know I would have given in to what they wanted, and I think Lucas would have, too. Together, we knew we had to have some time for ourselves, some privacy, some space from the constant pressure of chores and farm.

"I fantasize at night," I said.

Lucas was very interested in that.

"No, no. About lipstick. Hot showers. Car exhaust fumes. Nightclubs. Offices. Crowds of people."

"They're out there."

"Isn't it odd, Lucas? For our parents *out there* is horrible. For us, *out there* is everything we want."

"Not quite everything," said Lucas, taking me in his arms.

"What would you do, Lucas, if you were out of here?"

"Go to college. Learn everything I could. Spend four years thinking about what I'd do. How about you?"

"I don't know. One thing I can say definitely. When it comes to the future, I am always confused."

"Sometimes I think I actually would come back to the farm. Maybe I just want the decision to be mine and not my parents'."

"*You'd come back here?*"

Lucas half nodded and half shrugged. "I enjoy it, Marnie. I'm good at it. Do you know I'm a better farmer than either of Mr. Shields' sons, and they grew up on a farm. I have a knack for it. I love some of it."

I was amazed.

"I like so much else, though, too," he said. "I'd like to figure out a way to have the best of two worlds."

"Mother and Dad don't think that's possible. They say you have to choose."

"I think they're wrong," said Lucas, sighing. "But to prove it, I'd have to get away on my own for a few years, go back to school, have time to look around, try things, experiment."

Lucas' wood business grew and grew. A surprising number of people horrified by oil prices had put small woodstoves in their living rooms and few had their own sources of wood. By the end of winter, anybody who had started out with his own wood had long since burned it.

Since I was in school during the week, Lucas delivered Saturdays and Sundays, so I could go with him. We'd load a cord of wood into the wagon. Drive it to the buyer's. Unload and restack it. Collect the money. I wore thick brown cotton gloves to protect my hands. Lucas rarely wore gloves. His hands were leathery enough.

Once we went roller skating at an arena twenty-nine miles away. Neither of us had ever skated before. It had become a craze since we left the real world. We spent most of the time on our bottoms, but it wasn't humiliating because we were together. In fact, I think we were the envy of the rest of the teenagers, who skated beautifully, because we were having so much fun.

"Disco lights?" said my mother in genuine pain. "Rock music? When we need money for insulating this house? How could you?"

"I need to be with Lucas," I said. "Don't you remember? We talked about it once. Being in love. All the nice small things."

"Yes, I remember," she said more softly. "I'm sorry, honey. I'm not trying to ram things down your throat, really I'm not. It's hard for me to see you as a young woman who wants different things, obviously, than I want for you."

"Lucas?" I said. "Don't you want Lucas for me?"

Yes, she did. But she wanted us with her, at the farm, not by ourselves, "out" somewhere that she felt was second best.

Lucas opened a savings account and put in what he got from every third sale.

"How much have you saved so far?" I said.

"Ah, Marnie, don't even ask. All that sweat and hauling, and I've got a lousy four hundred twenty dollars. Enough money to get me somewhere, but not enough to do anything for me once I get there."

"You could get a job."

"Sure, I could. But I've got a job right now. I want school. Tell me how I'm going to pay for college. Buy books. Pay fees. Tuition. Room and board. Find time to study and go to labs while I'm holding down this job with the skills I don't have."

I couldn't tell him. I didn't know.

Chapter XVI

The second winter drew slowly to a close. Spring came, swiftly this year, reaching its beautiful peek and vanishing into summer before April was over.

I got to go to a prom with Lucas after all, my own. Nobody ever looked so handsome in a tuxedo as Lucas did. Our parents didn't mention the cost of renting one. Mother made me a beautiful dress, close-fitting, with a dipping neckline I had thought she would take out of the pattern. I felt like a princess.

"I'd feel like a prince myself," said Lucas, "except my nose reminds me the last thing I hauled in this bus was manure."

"Keep sniffing your gardenia. It'll keep your mind off that sort of thing."

But we had not realized what people would talk about on prom night. Each other, of course, and the years at high school, and who was with whom, and how everybody looked.

But mostly, what we were going to do next. Secretarial school, army, working in a parent's store, plumber's apprentice — and college. Everybody in my crowd was going to college. "What are you going to do, Marnie?" they said.

"Farming," I said.

"Farming," said Lucas.

Nobody was interested in that. We'd always done that. They wanted to talk about college. About going places and doing things and learning things. About which school had better engineering classes and which was best for elementary education.

The prom was Saturday night.

When Lucas and I met at breakfast Sunday morning, the house was empty. Our parents must be out working somewhere, I thought, and I suggested a picnic breakfast to Lucas.

We fixed a thermos of coffee (a recent splurge of Uncle Bob's) and a jar of homemade — what else? — applesauce, some of my sweet rolls and napkins. Out the window we spotted our parents.

"They're deciding whether to put in more herbs this year, I bet," said Lucas. "Mother was thinking she might be able to sell herb vinegar or something."

Quietly and carefully we walked out the front door so they wouldn't see us. Not that we were off to do anything wrong, but people who are up and moving in our house get chores to do, and we both felt the need to talk instead.

The geese honked the way they do for me, but

nobody yelled after us, and we went over the meadows, up the hill to our favorite picnic spot under a sourwood tree.

We had just sat down and opened the themos when five goats joined us. Lucas swore. I had forgotten to shut the gate behind us. I didn't blame him for being furious. There is nothing harder to catch than a playful goat. You can sit still and hope he'll get curious about you, but that rarely works five goats in a row.

One goat had its collar on, so I grabbed her and Lucas manhandled another, using his belt for a collar. We got those two down to the barnyard, shoved them in, rounded up some escaping hens, and caught the cow halfway across the pasture that would have led her into the flowerbed. Then we ran up the hill again, this time with ropes, to get the other three goats.

"I think," said Lucas, puffing, "that those goats want out just as much as we do."

"Some old film buff should be here," I said, leaping unsuccessfully after an agile young nannie.

"Why?" panted Lucas.

We both slipped, catching each other instead of the goat between us which would have been fine, except we really did have to catch the silly goats. "We must look like something out of Laurel and Hardy, that's why."

It took us half an hour to get the last goat and haul him down to the barnyard and close the gate on him. "Lucas!" yelled his father. "Work to do!"

We hesitated. There was work to do, a lot of it,

and we'd wasted so much time because of my carelessness. "I've got something to fetch up on the hill," yelled Lucas back. "I'll be with you as soon as I can."

We trudged back up the hill. "Climbing up gets less romantic each time," said Lucas.

"I noticed."

We flopped down on the grass. After a bit I poured us each a cup of coffee that was still nicely hot.

"Do you know what we'd be doing right now if we still lived in the city?" said Lucas.

"Let's see. Sunday morning after a big night out. We'd be reading the *Times*. We'd be ready to start the crossword puzzle."

"No. We'd be perusing the catalog of the college of our choice. Deciding whether to take Economics One or Oriental Literature. And whether to take these at nine A.M., thus leaving insufficient time for sleeping late, or at noon, thereby cutting into our carefully arranged program of television soap operas."

"Anxiously awaiting the mail, to see if Basket-weaving has been filled and we have to take freshman English after all."

"Wondering about the really big decisions. Like whether to join a fraternity."

It was impossible to believe people were still out there worrying about social acceptance when I had to go down the hill to clean kerosene lamps, haul water, handwash a load of laundry filthy from our slipping in the mud of spring rains.

"Which fraternity are you joining?" I asked.

"I thought maybe Tri-Goat."

We laughed hysterically.

"Marnie," said Lucas. "I've had enough. I'm ready to go."

I looked at him uncertainly.

"I don't want to plant another seed, spray another apple, or catch another goat."

It wasn't our usual shared complaining. It was a calm statement of fact. A shiver ran up my back. Lucas meant it. He was ready to leave.

"You want to go with me?" he said. I could hardly hear his voice. I touched his cheek and both of us forgot how to breathe.

"You know what a fraternity guy does," he said, "when he wants to show a girl he likes her best?"

"Mother says we can't do that. We aren't that free."

"Not that, Marnie. You don't have to be in a fraternity to do that, believe me. No, fraternity guys have these little gold pins, and they pin them on the girl's sweater, and that proclaims to the campus that they're pledged to each other."

I thought of the goats and the chores. "I don't think our campus is interested."

Lucas reached into his hip pocket and pulled out something shiny.

"A safety pin?" I said.

"It's all I have." He pinned the tiny metal strip on my blue chambray work shirt.

"If there one thing we know about, Marnie, it's work. We've put in two years reclaiming this orchard and getting this farm going. There has to be something out there that we can earn a living at. I'll put you through school and you put me through. Is it a deal, or do I rip my pin from your blouse?"

We held each other and I could feel the tiny hard line of the safety pin between his chest and mine.

"It would hurt them," I said.

"I don't think so. They won't need us so much this year as they did the others."

That was true. Routines were easier now, chores less exhausting or confusing. Impossible tasks had been dropped, intensely disliked jobs refined.

"Besides," said Lucas, "I'm nineteen and you're eighteen. Old enough to make a decision together. Our parents moved here for our sakes as well as for theirs, and I guess I really am grateful to them for it. It did us a lot of good. But it's spring, Marnie, and in the spring — "

"And in the spring," I said, laughing, "a young man's fancy turns to thoughts of love."

"Darn right. This young man's fancy has also turned to college and jobs and money, and I wouldn't mind a goat shortage at all."

Spring. Two Aprils ago, my parents had dragged me away from everything I thought had counted. One April ago, I was in love with a boy who didn't know I existed. This April, he loved me.

April is a time for new beginnings, I thought. And our beginning will have to be different from our parents'.

"It's a deal, Lucas," I said.

We packed up the picnic things and walked back to the farmhouse, hand in hand, to tell our parents we loved them, we loved what they had done for our sakes, but we loved each other, too, and things would have to be different.

The wind riffled our hair, the sun glinted off my safety pin, and somewhere out there, a world was waiting.